MISTLETOE SCANDAL

SYLVIA MCDANIEL

VIRTUAL BOOKSELLER LLC

❀ Created with Vellum

Mistletoe, Montana Where Kisses Lead to Happily Ever After.

After a devastating tragedy, Everleigh Walsh's uncle insists she come to Mistletoe, Montana to celebrate Christmas. Trying to deal with the horrible events she left behind, she is stunned to discover her uncle's neighbor, cowboy Seth Ketchum, waiting for her at the train station. Just when Everleigh decides life can't get any more complicated, an unexpected blizzard forces her and Seth to seek shelter in the most unlikely place - his home!

Being left at the altar, Seth moved to Mistletoe, Montana to escape the female sex. His plans to avoid women are waylaid when an unexpected accident forces him to help his friend and neighbor, James Walsh. Caught in a wintery storm, he quickly curses his chivalrous offer to escort Walsh's niece to his friend's ranch.

The weather seals them together in Seth's warm, cozy cabin, causing sparks to fly between him and the lovely Everleigh. Two broken lives are thrust together, caught in a winter wonderland where they must decide if they can build a future together or weather the scandal. Can the magic of a mistletoe kiss change their minds?

CHAPTER 1

$\mathcal{M}$istletoe, Montana, December 12, 1890

CONFIRMED bachelor Seth Ketchum stood waiting at the train station for a woman he didn't know--had no intention of know-ing--whose train was two hours late in the small town of Mistle-toe. All because James Walsh, a friend, had been gored by Seth's bull. One thing was certain: you didn't want to get between a bovine and his heifer.

Maybe Seth should feel grateful. He'd gotten three new calves because of the twelve hundred pounds of horny beef, but that came at the price of being chased out of his own pasture more than once. And now James was laid up because he'd helped Seth. Picking up his niece from the train station was the least he could do to make it up to his neighbor.

Glancing around at the small town, the ten buildings that made up the little village, he couldn't help but think about his own brothers and sisters and wonder how they were all getting along. He missed them, but not enough to return to Oregon.

"Seth," the preacher Bart Nichols called, waving at him from across the street. Dodging wagons and horses, he crossed the snow covered lane, shivering in his suit coat and tie. "Good morning, son. I was wondering if you were picking up Miss Walsh?"

Seth eyed the man and nodded. He'd been raised in the church. His mother was the daughter of a preacher who had traveled to Oregon. Unfortunately, his grandfather had been killed by Indians along the way.

"Yes, sir. I told James not to worry. I'd meet her train and get her out to his place."

"That's awfully good of you," he said. "I know James has been worried about her. This is her first holiday without her family."

"He told me," Seth said, looking off to the north watching the sky. "I just wish her train would get here so we could get going. I don't like the looks of those clouds."

The preacher glanced in that direction. "Yes, and the temperature seems to be dropping. Maybe both of you should stay in town. I'd hate for you to get stranded on the road somewhere."

"Can't. I have stock out at the ranch that need tending."

Winter was upon them and he wouldn't let his animals starve while he sat in a hotel waiting for the roads to clear enough to get home. No, he wanted to leave now, but would wait another thirty minutes and then he would have no choice but to return home.

"Understand, son. Just be careful," he said. "Getting home is not worth freezing to death."

Montana winters had already schooled him once on the severity of the cold and snow. The very first year, he learned quickly that when the sky darkened, it was best to make certain you had a rope tied to the barn, because a man could get turned around quickly when he couldn't see anything but swirling snowflakes. It was why he wished that train would arrive.

"Here comes the train," the preacher said. "Now, let me introduce her to you since she doesn't know you."

"She doesn't know you either," he said, staring at him like he'd lost his mind.

The owner of the newspaper, Tom Stuart, walked up beside them. "Preacher, Seth, is this the train Miss Walsh is arriving on?"

"We hope so," Seth said, wondering about the contraption hanging around his neck. He thought it was a camera, but he wasn't sure. He'd never seen one that wasn't on a stand.

"Great, I want to interview her for the paper," he said smiling. "It's not every day we get visitors from New York City here in Mistletoe. And besides, I need some holiday news."

The wind suddenly gusted, sending ice and snow blowing, stinging Seth's face. "We don't have time for an interview. I've got to get her out to her aunt and uncle's before the weather turns bad."

He was feeling as nervous as a cat, right now. His stomach clenched with anxiety and pressure to get on the road. They'd already had snow several times this winter and being the start of the second week of December, the weather could change in no time from sunny to snowy.

Tom ignored him and stood staring at the incoming train.

The train pulled to a halt in front of the depot and they watched as the passengers disembarked, one by one. Finally, a beautiful woman with silky dark auburn hair alighted, laughing and flirting with a man who held out his hand for her to disembark. Seth rolled his eyes.

That had to be her.

His chest tightened at the sight of the gorgeous woman with long limbs, a small waist, and curvaceous breasts. He knew what every man here was thinking as she looked around the station for her uncle. They all wanted to rescue her, save her, and keep her for themselves, but he had the responsibility of making certain she arrived safely at her uncle's house.

"Miss Walsh," the preacher said, hurrying toward her, his short, fat legs scrambling to reach the beauty.

She turned toward him and smiled. "Yes?"

"I'm Bart Nichols, the preacher here in Mistletoe, and we'd like to welcome you to our little town. Unfortunately, your uncle couldn't make it. He was gored by a bull last week."

"Oh no. Is he going to be all right?" she said, her large green eyes widening with concern. "Everleigh Walsh," she said, sticking out her hand. "How is my uncle doing?"

"He'll be fine. He was lucky the bull got him in the thigh."

Guilt flooded Seth, gripping his stomach. The damn fool animal was mean and ornery and only good for making baby cows. If he didn't need the animal, he would shoot him for being so contrary.

Seth shook his head at the spectacle the preacher was making of himself fawning all over a pretty young woman. Sure, women were in high demand in the new state of Montana, but he was a married man. A man of the cloth. A holy man.

"How will I get out to his place? He told me it's an hour from town," she asked, her eyes growing large in her beautiful, round face with high cheekbones and full, ripe lips ready to be kissed.

"Seth has agreed to see you to your uncle's," he said, taking her by the arm and walking her down the steps of the depot to the street where they waited.

Leaning against his sled with his arms folded across his chest, he watched the woman coming toward him. He knew her type. She was fanciful and bold and knew the effect she had on men. He'd seen women like her use their control of men and even experienced their effects himself. After all, he'd been left waiting at the altar by a woman like her. The very reason he'd moved to Montana.

He would deliver Miss Walsh and then drive home to the safety of his ranch. Staying away from James and his family until his niece left town.

"Miss Walsh," the newspaper man said, hurrying toward her.

"Welcome to Mistletoe. May I take your picture for the newspaper?"

"Why, of course," she said.

The preacher posed with Miss Walsh, smiling into the camera as the newspaper man lifted the fancy gadget around his neck to his face. With a pop and a flash, the camera took the photo.

Seth glanced uneasily at the sky. They didn't have time for this nonsense. They needed to get on the road or face a very cold, snowy drive.

"How long are you visiting your uncle?" Tom asked.

"I have to return to New York after the first of the year," she said.

Seth chuckled. Had anyone ever told this woman that sometimes the trains didn't run because of snow on the tracks? She'd be doing good to get a train out of here in January.

"What about your parents?" the reporter asked. "Why didn't they accompany you to Mistletoe?"

Seth watched as her face seemed to freeze, her body visibly tightening. She swallowed and tried to smile, but her eyes filled with pain, and he wanted to hit that stupid newspaper man. James had warned him not to discuss her parents as their deaths were recent and now this idiot was asking about her family. He needed to get her out of here.

The preacher was glaring at Tom like he was the biggest fool.

"My parents were killed, six months ago. My uncle invited me to spend the holidays with his family so I wouldn't be alone," she said. "Excuse me, gentlemen, but I need to collect my trunk."

"I'll get it," Seth said, stepping away from the sled. He walked up to her. "Seth Ketchum, ma'am. I'll take you to your uncle's."

"Thank you," she said, her voice a throaty softness, almost a purr that sent a tingle to the base of his spine. Oh no, he wasn't letting this beauty get to him. "Everleigh Walsh."

"We best be going. That blue cloud, I fear, is a blizzard and we need to get on the road."

She hesitated. "All right, Mr. Ketchum. My trunk is the brown one sitting on the dock."

After he walked away, he heard her ask the preacher, "Is it safe to ride alone with him? I mean it's almost an hour there."

The preacher patted her on the arm. "Seth is a fine young man. He'll protect your honor."

The woman didn't want to be alone with him anymore than he wanted to drive her to her uncle's. But he felt obligated since he was the reason her uncle was hurt and it was only for an hour. Then the deed would be done.

Out of the corner of his eye, Seth watched her nervously bite her lip, watching him as he lifted her trunk off the dock and carried it to the sleigh he'd driven into town. Dropping it into the back, he glanced at the newspaper man scribbling notes on a piece of paper.

"Miss Walsh, what are your plans while you're visiting Mistletoe," he asked.

"To visit with my aunt and uncle."

The newspaper man's questions were ridiculous and wasting time. It was time to go.

"What about the future? What are your plans after you leave here?" he asked.

Everleigh smiled and the men around her stared in adoration. "I'm going to work for the *New York Times*."

Seth looked at her. Oh yeah, she was exactly what he thought. A highfalutin woman who wanted a career.

"Let's go," he said, waiting to help her into the sleigh.

She continued to talk to the newspaper man while the sun was being obliterated by clouds rolling across the sky. Most definitely, a storm.

They should have been on the road an hour ago. "Let's go."

She ignored him. He walked around to his side of the sleigh, got in, and snapped the reins. The sleigh started to pull away.

"Wait," she called, suddenly springing into action hurrying after him.

That had gotten her attention. He stopped the sleigh. "You ready to leave now?"

Frowning at him, she climbed into the sleigh. "Shut up and let's go."

CHAPTER 2

*E*verleigh couldn't believe the audacity of this man. He was going off without her. Leaving her behind because she'd been busy talking to the nice man from the newspaper. A woman could never be too sure of a man's temperament. Men were known for their carnal natures. They liked to be in control of everyone and everything and when he'd started off without her, it was just another example of men and their attempt to discipline a woman.

"As soon as my conversation was finished, I was going to leave with you," she said in a snit.

The man was insufferable. He would have left her. The other two men had seemed so nice and sincere while Mr. Smarty Pants had been standing off, distant and aloof, and handsome as sin on a stick. So sure of himself and how he was going to dominate everything like he was king of the new state of Montana with his coal black hair and big blue eyes that seemed so doubtless and confident.

"Do you see those dark clouds in the distance?" he said coolly, not even turning to glance at her.

"Yes, it looks like rain. What has that got to do with anything?"

"Honey, this time of year, we don't get rain. We get snow. If we're going to make it to your aunt and uncle's, we should have been on the road over an hour ago."

The way he said *honey* was not an endearment, but more sarcastic and arrogant. Like he thought she was the stupidest female in the area.

"The train was late."

"Understood. But the time for chitchatting about nothing was over. It was time to get on the road," he said, his eyes never leaving the snow-covered path.

The man must not have a heart or a soul as she could see. He was cold and authoritative. Just what she didn't need or want in any man.

Turning away from him, she concentrated on the route they traveled. Pine trees loaded with snow lined the winding road, reminding her of home. Soon, she'd be with the only family she had left, missing her mother and father more than before. How Mr. Smarty Pants knew where he was going, she didn't know except for maybe the tracks of other sleds and horses' hooves.

"There's a fur pelt in the back. I suggest you pull it up and wrap it around you. It's going to get cold," he told her.

Since they'd left the train station, she'd felt the wind whipping about her, making her wish she'd worn more layers of clothing.

"Even colder than it already is? I can't feel my toes."

"Wrap the pelt around you."

She glared at him. Was he always so bossy? She wanted to ignore him, but her feet were frigid and the wind was picking up and it was already blowing briskly against her in the sleigh. Her toes were starting to numb, and any kind of warmth, right now, would feel really good. Reluctantly, like she wasn't feeling the piercing wind a bit, she reached back and nonchalantly pulled the pelt from the back. An animal fur. She shivered at this point wondering what poor animal gave up his skin for them to have warmth. Turning back, snowflakes hit her cheek.

He cursed.

"Excuse me," she said to let him know she'd heard his foul language.

He glanced at her. "I was hoping we'd make it to your uncle's before the snow started. But we're only ten minutes out of town and already the flakes are flying. We could be in trouble."

What was he talking about? It was snow. They had snow in New York. Even heavy snowfall that paralyzed the city at least once a year. Right now, the sight of white flakes falling gently from the sky was beautiful. She stuck out her tongue and grabbed one with a giggle. With the pine trees already glistening white, the new flakes just made the world look like an ice palace, all bright pearly and gleaming.

"Why do you think we're in trouble?"

He glanced at her and grimaced. "We're heading into a blizzard, lady. A frigid, snowy storm that is going to make the road harder and harder to see. Where I can't tell where the road stops and starts. Where we could get lost and wander around until we're frozen."

The man was an alarmist. A person who liked to prophesy gloom and doom and calamities. And she was going to spend the next hour on pins and needles wondering if they were going to make it to her uncle's. Of course, they would arrive.

Shaking her head, she glanced at him. "And how long have you lived in Montana?"

"Three years. Long enough to know a blizzard when I see one and realize the danger."

Opening her reticule, she pulled out her father's pocket watch and glanced at the time. He'd given it to her so she wouldn't be late the night she'd left the apartment to meet her fiancé for dinner. It was the night her father died. The night she should have died if not for her disastrous dinner date. A date that went from bad to worse in a matter of moments.

"Look, Mr..."

"Seth Ketchum."

"Look, Seth, I didn't escape an explosion in New York City to come to Montana to die. So stop acting like the end is near and get this sleigh to my uncle's."

As if the weather had heard her defiance, the wind slashed the sleigh and the horse neighed in alarm.

Frozen pellets pelted her face.

"Yes, ma'am," he said sarcastically. "But that there gust of wind is a clear indication we're heading into a blizzard."

"Then get us to my aunt and uncle's as soon as possible," she said, a tiny prickle of worry starting to zig along her spine. Like she said, she was not going to die in some freak blizzard in Montana.

The snow fell faster and thicker, and at times, she wondered how he could even see the road. The horse seemed to have slowed, it's head down, but he trotted on like he knew where he was going. Her fingers were starting to numb and she tucked the fur around her closer, no longer caring it was a dead animal skin keeping her warm.

Thirty minutes later, she'd moved the scarf that was around her neck up to her face, protecting her cheekbones from the stinging ice that felt like needles. The vista was no longer beautiful, and she counted minutes, hoping they would soon arrive. She worried they would pass her uncle's house in the swirling white, never seeing the home.

"How m-much further?" she asked, screaming into the wind.

"We're not even half way," he said, glancing around them. "I'm having to remember trees and bushes along the road, but in the snow, it all looks different."

Moaning in frustration, she ducked her head to try to keep the cold wind at bay.

Suddenly Seth stopped the sleigh and hopped out.

"What-t-t are you doing," she asked, her voice quivering, her body wracked by penetrating shivers. She'd never take feeling warm for granted again. "Let's-s-s go," she cried, her voice shaking.

Ignoring her, he walked up to the horse and held his hand over the horse's nose and rubbed his head. Then he hurried back to the sleigh. "The horse had too much frost and snow caking his nose. I had to wipe it off." He glanced at her. "Are you doing all right?"

"I'mm....f-freezing," she said, shivering, her teeth clattering.

"I know. Me, too," he said. Suddenly he grabbed her by the arm and pulled her close to him.

"Stop. What-t-t...are...you...d-doing?" she protested, but it came out sounding weak.

"We're sharing body heat," he said. He took the pelt and wrapped it around the two of them. An infusion of heat and warmth from his body felt wonderful. Taking a deep breath, she breathed in his scent and her heart beat a little faster at the feel of his hard muscled thigh rubbing against her skirts. She should move away, but she was too cold.

"I don't think we're going to make it to your uncle's," he said quietly. "The storm is getting worse. I can't tell where we're at."

She glanced at him, her facial movements feeling frozen. "Where will we stop?"

"My house is about ten minutes up the road. We're going there."

"No," she demanded. "I want-t t-to keep going."

"You want to die?" he asked.

"No, but..."

"Then we're going to my house until this blizzard blows over."

Everleigh wanted to kick and scream and demand that he take her to her uncle's, but part of her knew they were making the right decision. In fact, a sensible voice in her head said they would be lucky to make it to his place. The wind was howling so hard and fast, she couldn't see anything but white in front of her. Thank goodness the horse seemed to sense they were close to home and turned down a frosted lane lined with drifts.

Finally, after what seemed like forever, the horse stopped. The snow was blowing so hard, she could barely make out a structure.

Seth turned to her. "Wait. Let me help you. You're wet and cold."

The rashness of this man. She could get out of the sleigh without his help. She threw off the pelt and regretted her action the moment she did. The frigid air blasted her and she realized how much colder it would have been without that blanket of warmth. Throwing her stiff leg over the side of the sleigh, she stepped down and immediately fell face first into a deep drift. She couldn't feel her limbs. They were numb from the arctic chill and she lay there struggling to move in the snowbank.

"You just couldn't wait, could you?" he said, lifting her.

"I am quite capable of taking care of myself."

"I can see that," he said, swinging her body into his arms.

"What are you doing?" she asked, feeling breathless being held by this lumbering hunk of a man.

"I'm carrying you into the house."

A sense of warmth and security enveloped her as he carried her one hundred ten pounds of frozen humanity. When they walked inside, he set her gently on the ground.

"Can you stand?"

"I think so," she said, grabbing onto a chair and looking around, her feet still frozen. "Where is your family?"

Lighting a lantern, he fussed with the lamp until it was lit. As light spread throughout the house, he glanced at her and then licked his lips. "I live alone."

For a moment, she felt a thousand needles stinging her face and limbs. They were alone with a raging blizzard outside.

"I can't stay here."

"You have no choice," he said and walked out the door.

As the door closed, she sighed and let her head slump to her chest. She was alone with a surly man who didn't even like her.

CHAPTER 3

*S*eth rushed out of the house and into the snowy cold where he'd left the horse and sleigh. The bitter cold was a welcome respite from the sharp tongued greenhorn from New York. The woman could be trying and now they were stuck together. The horse made a deep rumble in his chest.

"I know, Rusty, it's bitter out here. Give me just a moment and you'll be in the barn with a nice fresh bag of oats," he said, locating the rope he had tied to the house. He stretched it out, walking into the swirls of white, unable to see the barn, but knowing it was close. He bumped into the building, kicking his frozen toes against the wood. "Found it."

Walking along the building, he located the door and tied the rope to the handle. Now he could come and go between the the two buildings without getting lost. Snapping a throat hook onto the rope, the other end he tied to his belt. Quickly, he made his way back to the sled.

"Let's get you in the barn," he told the horse. It must sound crazy, but he talked to his animals all the time. They were usually the only breathing creatures around for miles. Except now Everleigh occupied his house, filling it with her womanly scent and gorgeous..."Stop, right there."

It wouldn't do him any good to be thinking about the curves hidden under that fancy dress she was wearing. She was so far above of a rancher's league.

Climbing into the sleigh, he turned the vehicle in the direction of where he thought the barn was and the horse gladly pulled him right up to the door, which he pulled open with the rope attached to his waist. With little urging, the horse trotted inside where he climbed down.

"Hey, Big Blue," he said, reaching down and petting the mutt he'd raised from a pup. The dog licked his hand. "We've got a guest, so you can't come up to the house."

The dog whined like he understood his owner.

Quickly, he went to work unharnessing the horse. He glanced around at the animals curled up nice and warm inside the building. A milk cow, a couple of calves, some chickens, a few grunting pigs, and three horses. Most of his cattle were in the pasture not far from the house and he prayed they would make it through the storm. He hated to think of them out there in this weather. As soon as it stopped snowing, he'd be taking them hay. The stock hay was safely inside the new sheds he'd built in the pasture this summer, but he still went out and spread the hay bales for his cattle.

Once he'd brushed and fed the horse, he glanced toward the house and thought of the woman waiting for him there. He was tempted to sleep out here in the barn. If people in town learned they'd spent the night alone, no matter what the circumstances, no matter that nothing happened between them, they would be required to marry. Even James might insist he marry his niece.

And good Lord, he didn't want that woman tied to him forever. He'd gotten lucky once and while it hadn't been his doing, he now knew he was much better off without the girl he'd been engaged to.

Sighing, he knew he should go in. The woman didn't have sense enough to know she'd just survived a blizzard. And that her wet clothes would only make her sick. He was going to look like the biggest pervert demanding she take them off and hang them up to dry. But he didn't need her catching pneumonia and dying at his place. Or her uncle blaming him for her illness.

He was in quite a pickle. One demanding, beautiful, sexy as hell woman having to stay in his home unchaperoned. He wondered if she realized the consequences of them being snowed in alone together.

Walking into the house, the first thing he noticed was her squatted beside his fireplace, a blanket tossed about her shoulders.

"Oh, come on, light," she said, striking the flint at paper she'd stuffed under a log.

Feeling remorse for not making a fire before he went to the barn, he strode over to the fireplace. "Let me."

Standing, she bumped into him, her breast brushing against his arm. His cold blood heated, rushing through him. Licking his dry lips, he leaned down and struck the flint. A spark hit the paper, igniting it.

"You make it look so easy," she said.

"I've had more practice than you," he responded, not looking at her.

Within a matter of moments, the fire was blazing and heat warmed the room. "I got busy taking care of the animals in the barn."

It wasn't exactly an apology, but more an explanation.

"I couldn't find a kettle, but I found a pan. Do you have tea?"

He swallowed. He'd never had a woman in his home. Hell, he had very few visitors. "No tea. But I have coffee."

"As long as it's warm, it will do," she said. She started to sit, but instantly jumped up when she realized the back of her dress was soaked. She went to the fire and turned her backside to the flame.

"You need to get out of those wet clothes. I'm going to change as well."

She glared at him. "And just what do you think I'm going to change into? All my clothes are packed away in my trunk. And where is my trunk?"

Seth sighed. He hadn't even thought about unloading her baggage. She wasn't supposed to be here. She wasn't supposed to stay. Sometime soon, very soon, he was going to need to retrieve her trunk from the barn. For now, she could put on his clothes...if she would.

Crossing his arms over his chest, he stared at her, knowing she wasn't going to like what he had to say.

"I'm not going back out in that snow. I'm cold. I'm tired. You can wear one of my pants and a shirt."

She stared at him, her mouth opening in shock. "*Your* clothes!" Her voice rose. "You want me to wear your clothes?"

"Or you can go without," he said sarcastically, the words slipping into the open. He watched her bristle. Maybe he shouldn't have said that.

"You need to take me to my uncle's, right now. That was a crude suggestion and I will not accept your insolence."

He laughed. "Lady, the only way you're getting to your uncle's tonight is if you walk."

"Fine. I will."

He watched in disbelief as she put on her coat, hat, and gloves and went to the door. When she turned the knob, the door flew out of her hands and smacked the wall, the force of the wind blowing snow into the house and chilling the room instantly. She stood there a moment, her mouth open. The storm had grown stronger.

Walking over to her, he shoved the door shut and latched it.

"'Tis not a fit night for man or beast. If you want to walk to your uncle's, that's your choice, but before you go, I insist you write out your last will and testament."

She turned and stared at him in shock. "You are no gentleman."

He shrugged. "Probably not. My mother used to tell me I was a trying child."

Putting her hands over her face, she sighed heavily and shook her head. "This is going to ruin my reputation. We can't stay here alone without a chaperone. There's no one here but us."

"Maybe we can get you to your uncle's and no one will know."

She glanced up at him, her emerald eyes wide with fright. "I won't tell."

"I won't tell," he assured her. "I don't like this situation any more than you do."

Sighing, she stared at him, her eyes narrowing. "You did this on purpose."

The woman was crazy. "What? Create a blizzard so I'm trapped here with you?" Shaking his head. "If you remember, I was the one trying to get you to come on while you chitchatted with the newspaper man."

The reality of their situation hit her and he had the urge to comfort her, but stood his ground afraid she would think ill of him if he touched her.

"Look, we can't change things. We just have to accept what's happened and try to make the best of the situation. Maybe no one will ever know," he said softly. "I'd offer to sleep in the barn, but that's not going to matter. No one is going to believe that we didn't..."

"Ohh, believe me, I'll know we didn't," she said.

He laughed, easing the tension knowing this was going to be a long night. "You can have the bedroom and I'll sleep out here on the couch. That way I can keep the fire going all night and hopefully, we'll stay warm."

This really wasn't fair to either of them. In order to survive, they had to share a residence alone. He only hoped her uncle understood and didn't force him into a shotgun wedding.

She shook her head. "I don't have a nightgown. I have nothing in here with me."

"I should have thought about your trunk. But frankly, I was just thrilled to get us safely to the house. That last mile, I was worried we weren't going to make it." He gazed at her. "I'll get you a pair of my pants and a shirt. We'll hang your dress next to the fire and hopefully by morning, it'll be dry."

"Do you think we can make it to my uncle's in the morning?"

Gazing at her, he could see fear on her beautiful face and wanted to somehow reassure her that she was safe with him, and he would get her home as soon as possible, but this blizzard was packing a nasty punch.

"We'll do our best," he said, walking into his bedroom. For her sake, and his, he hoped so, but there were no guarantees and the way the wind was howling, he feared this storm was one for the record books.

CHAPTER 4

*E*verleigh stood in his chilly bedroom after the door had closed and glanced around. It wasn't a bad room. In fact, it was cleaner than she'd expected. Small, neat, and organized. She gazed down at the clothes he'd laid on the bed for her. A man's pair of pants and a dark shirt. Shivering, she knew he was right. Being cold in these wet clothes could not be good for her, but neither could running around in a man's shirt and pants. They didn't even know one another and she was going to be wearing clothing that was more revealing than her dresses.

Reaching behind her, she struggled to undo the buttons on her dress. There was no way she was going out there and asking him to unbutton her clothing. That would be like asking him to take her to bed.

She shivered. When the top two buttons were loose, she pulled the wet garment up and tugged it over her breasts where it clung to her. Oh my, she was stuck, with no one to help. She'd stay tangled in her clothes forever before she would call him to help her. With a ripping sound the garment finally came over her head, knocking the pins from her hair. "Oh, fiddlesticks."

"You okay in there?" he called.

Quickly, she held the dress in front of her in case he opened the door, her heart beating in her chest. "Fine."

Sinking onto the bed, she looked at the seam she'd ripped. With a little ingenuity it could be fixed.

What was she doing here?

Taking a deep breath, she released the nerves that threatened to overwhelm her. She reminded herself she was a suffragette, a fighter for women to have the right to own property, have a bank account, custody of their children, and even vote.

During college, she'd marched with women for the right to vote. She'd been a very young woman, but they'd thrown her in jail just like all the others. For hours, they'd sat on the concrete floor, singing and talking and laughing and doing everything they could to drive the jailers nuts. After that experience, she could handle one night with a man she didn't know, wearing his clothes.

Jerking her shoulders back, she thought of her friends in New Hope, Texas, several of them married and Abigail expecting a baby. For Christmas, she should have gone to Texas rather than Montana.

Sighing, she removed her wet corset. Thank goodness in college she'd tossed her normal corset and started wearing the "Perfect Health" corset that she could easily remove herself.

As she put one leg into his pants, she smiled, trying to bolster her courage. If only her friends could see her now. They'd know she truly was a modern woman, wearing men's clothing and stranded alone. Her chin trembled as she fought back the tears. She could do this. She had no choice.

Tugging his shirt over her chemise, she sighed, then breathed in the smell of Seth as warmth filled her. Moving about the room, she couldn't help but feel the freedom of wearing pants, yet they were scratchy against her legs and tight.

Walking to the door, she felt naked, vulnerable, and nervous and reminded herself again, she could do this.

Yanking open the door to the bedroom, her stomach quivered as she glanced to Seth, determined not to let him make her feel more uncomfortable. Stepping out with her sodden garments in front of her like a shield, she hurried to a line he'd strung near the fireplace. Quickly, she hung the clothes where hopefully, they'd soon dry and she could put her dress back on.

Seth stood near the fire. His eyes widened as he skimmed her apparel. Clearing his throat, he swallowed.

"They look better on you than me," he said, his voice sounding gruff.

Awkwardly, she glanced at him, "Thanks, I guess."

He nodded toward the kitchen. "I made a fresh pot of coffee. I thought maybe it might warm you up."

"Thank you."

"There's cups on the shelf and sugar in the bowl," he said awkwardly. "I'll fix a pot of stew for supper, if that's okay?"

She nodded, unable to think about eating as she found the cups and fixed herself a mug of the hot brew. Turning, she picked up her coffee and came closer to the fire. A small couch sat in front, and she sank onto the sofa, feeling uncomfortable as the rough material of his pants scratched her tender thighs. The cotton shirt felt soft against her chemise and smelled like Seth. A warm, rich aroma of clean man. She licked her lips, her hands shaking from nerves that left her rattled.

"We have to reach my uncle's tomorrow."

"I'll do my best. But we wouldn't have survived in that snowstorm," he said, keeping his distance, standing off to the side of the fireplace.

He was right. She knew he was right, but she just hadn't wanted to give up. If she'd gone to Texas, at least there if they had snow, it wasn't life threatening and she would have been surrounded by women, not one lonely man who lived alone.

She knew nothing about this man and yet she had to trust him. Worse, she didn't think he even liked her. From the moment they met, he hadn't been friendly and had even tried to go off and leave her behind. Yet, now she understood why and wished she would have crawled into that sleigh the moment she got off the train.

"I'm sorry for dawdling at the train station," she said softly. "I had no idea it would be this bad."

Nodding was the only indication she received that he'd heard her. The man was insufferable. He spoke very little, only bobbing his head, not moving his mouth to the point she wanted to scream at him *"talk to me. Tell me what, if anything, you're thinking under that dark mop of gorgeous hair."* His blue eyes revealed more than his words, and even those, she sometimes had a hard time understanding their unspoken language.

She was tired. She was frustrated. She was still grieving, and now she was stuck in a cabin with a man she didn't know, who barely spoke while a snowstorm raged outside. Her reputation would be shattered from no fault of her own.

Tears rose in her eyes threatening to fall like an avalanche, the pain of the past months overwhelming her, causing her chest to ache from the unfairness of life. She should be home in New York with her family for Christmas. Her mother would be teasing her father and they would be sitting around the dinner table, talking about their day. Instead, she was here in this stupid little house, frightened and tired, and it was all too much.

To her horror, the first tear leaked out of her eye and then another, and another, and soon she covered her face and let the sobs rack her body. She shouldn't be here. She was Everleigh Walsh, suffragette, woman of the world, and instead she was reduced to a blubbering mess dressed in men's clothes, in a cabin with a strange male.

She wailed even louder, unable to stop the pain that engulfed her.

She felt his hand on her back and then he was pulling her into his arms laying her head on his shoulder. "Hey, what brought all this on? We're alive. We're safe."

Hiccupping, she tried to stop the tears. "For now. But once everyone learns we were alone tonight...they'll think...my reputation will be ruined." A new round of racking sobs hit her at the unfairness of the world.

She'd been a good girl her entire life and now because of a blizzard, she'd be shamed. It would be better if she'd died in that snowstorm than to spend the night with an unchaperoned man. At least then, she would have died with her reputation intact.

"If the snow stops falling, we'll go to your uncle's tomorrow. Maybe no one will think we spent the night alone. Your uncle would believe us if we tell him the truth that nothing happened."

She could feel her breasts squashed against his chest and his hand was rubbing her back as he held her in his arms. Tears ran unchecked down her cheeks soaking his shirt and her nose was running. She hated it when she cried, because now her face would be all red, her eyes swollen, and she'd have the sniffles.

"We can try," she said, her chest heaving. "But I'm afraid he'll insist we marry. You don't even like me."

More tears flowed from her eyes. Most people liked her. Most men adored her and yet the one man she was stuck with scorned her.

He sighed. "It's not that I don't like you. You remind me of someone who hurt me very badly."

Sniffling, she leaned back and gazed at him. "Your girlfriend?"

"Yes."

She wanted to ask him more questions, but he was staring at her lips, and for a moment, she thought he was going to kiss her. Suddenly, he placed his hands on her shoulder and leaned away.

She missed his nearness, the solidity of his chest, and the way she'd felt secure in his embrace. Did she want him to kiss her? Strong and handsome. Her pulse had accelerated the moment he touched her, but he barely talked.

"All better now?" he asked, moving away, putting distance between them.

Nodding, she glanced away. Seth Ketchum was a strong virile man who had captured her interest, but she was a newspaper journalist with a career waiting for her in New York. Her place was there, not here in the Montana wilderness.

CHAPTER 5

*T*he next morning, Seth laid on the couch, listening to the wind howl and rattle the shutters outside. The wind was blowing so hard that at times he feared the roof shingles were going to fly off. And the snow was still falling. He didn't know how much they'd received last night, but it had to be at least a foot if not more. The storm outside was nothing compared to the danger he realized he was in last evening.

Last night, holding Everleigh in his arms had been a mistake. The feel of her soft breasts crushed against his chest, the smell of roses and lavender swirling took him by surprise as his body reacted to her while she cried. And to think he'd been part of her anguish made his stomach tighten with pain. Sure, she looked and acted like Catherine, but she wasn't the same woman. If anything, she was more beautiful, more accomplished, and she was so far above him on the social scale, they couldn't even compare.

He was the product of a gambling man searching for his brother and a woman traveling with orphans to Oregon. His parents met when Indians attacked his mother's wagon train, killing everyone but her and the children who had gone down to the creek to get water, saving them.

His mother never let him forget that by the grace of God, he was walking on this earth, because she'd been spared from the attack. He loved and missed his family and leaving them behind had been the hardest thing he'd ever done. But circumstances had proven it was best if he left town and so he'd come to Mistletoe, Montana.

And now he loved his ranch, the small town, and the people here. He would never leave, so he had to ignore Everleigh's soft lips and the way she felt with her arms clinging to him as she cried.

The image of her curled up and sleeping in his bed was something he kept pushing out of his mind. The sight of her wearing his pants and shirt would haunt him forever. Her shapely, long limbs and perfectly curved butt filled out his pants in a way he could never imitate. While a storm raged outside, the woman was a temptation he had to endure, sleeping in the next room.

Without getting up and looking outside, he knew they would not be going to her uncle's today. Probably not even tomorrow, but he couldn't tell her that. And every minute he stayed with her, she would become more tempting than the last. Yet, what he was thinking was not a good idea. She had a life on the other side of America and his was here in Montana.

Sitting up, knowing he might as well rise and tend to the animals, he quickly donned his pants, shoving his shirt tails inside. He threw another log on the fire and stoked the small flame until it roared, heating the room. Just as he was about to head out to the barn, the door to the bedroom opened.

"Good morning. I didn't expect to see you this early," he said.

"Couldn't sleep," she replied, gazing at him, her luscious emerald eyes sleepy and somehow so alluring that he wanted to grab her and drag her back to the bedroom and do what he knew they would be accused of doing.

They stared at one another and she licked her lips and he wanted to groan.

"Why don't you fix some coffee while I tend to the animals," he said. The cold would be a welcome blast to tame the heat filling his body. He couldn't stay around her every minute of the day. He had to escape the sensual pull of her body.

"Are we going to my uncle's today?"

He hated to disappoint her, but he didn't think there was a chance in hell they could get down the road, even with the sleigh. "I haven't looked outside, but the wind is still howling."

Pulling his heavy coat and boots on, he bundled up and walked to the door. Yanking it open, he stared in stunned disbelief. The snow was halfway up the door and the wind blew a swirling mass of nothing but white. He couldn't see the barn.

Putting her hands over her face, she turned away. "I'm ruined."

The urge to take her in his arms was strong, but he couldn't. Not now. "Everleigh, fix some coffee and I'll be back soon. Then we'll talk about what we're going to do."

Sighing heavily, she faced him. "I'll have it ready when you come back. Be careful."

Warmth filled him as he smiled at her. "Always."

He hurried out the door, slamming it behind him, pushing through the drift.

She was right, but he wasn't ready to face the consequences of the weather. He didn't want to think about how her family would expect him to marry her. He wasn't prepared to have a wife that would hate living here in Montana and being a rancher's woman. He wasn't ready to think about marriage again.

CHAPTER 6

*E*verleigh glanced up from the coffee she'd been pouring when Seth walked in the door, carrying her trunk. She ran over to the opening and shut it after he struggled through.

"My trunk," she said happily following him into the bedroom, where he dropped her luggage. Without thinking, she threw her arms around him, ecstatic that her things were within reach and she could change out of his pants and shirt. The feel of his chest solid against her breasts had her realizing her mistake.

A stinging crackle of sensation along her spine had her catching and holding her breath. Quickly, she jumped, stumbling back and he grabbed her arm to keep her from falling onto the bed.

"Oh my," she said startled. "I guess, I got a little over excited."

They were standing in his room, the bed inches from them, staring at each other awkwardly, her heart hammering in her chest at the feel of his hand on her arm. The tight grip of heat flowed through her from his cold fingers.

"Your hands are like ice," she blundered, searching for something to say that would distract him from the sight of the rumpled sheets. The image of the two of them curled around one another in that bed had her heart *cathunking* in her chest like the roar of the train.

He released her.

"Yes," he said, a muscle in his jaw tightening, his eyes darkening with an emotion she'd never experienced. His body stiffened and he turned and walked out of the room.

She shut the door behind him and opened her trunk. Quickly, she changed her clothes, putting on a clean dress and undergarments. The only thing that would have made her feel better was a hot bath or him saying they were going to her uncle's. They had to try tomorrow; they just had to or she had no chance of saving her reputation.

After she finished pinning her hair on top of her head, she opened the door. Seth was in the kitchen cooking breakfast. "Do you like eggs?"

"Yes," she said as he turned to look at her.

Staring at her, his eyes skimmed her clothing. "Do you think we were going into town?"

For a moment, she stopped and gazed at him. Not a *you look nice*, or *that's pretty* or even *how do you like your eggs?* Instead, he was commenting on her choice of clothing. "Well, I thought after we went to the Smith's for tea, you might take me to that nice restaurant in town I've been wanting to eat at."

The expression on his face changed and his lips turned up in a smile as he laughed. "Either the cold has affected your sensibilities or the lady is quite good at sarcasm."

She shrugged. "You started it. Sorry my wardrobe is not fit for the Montana wilderness."

Nodding, he turned back to the pan on the stove.

"Do you have something wrong with your tongue?"

With a jerk, he glanced back at her. "What makes you ask?"

"Because conversation with you is ninety percent you nodding your head. So I thought maybe something was wrong with your tongue," she finally asked.

His eyes narrowed and she feared she'd made him angry.

Concentrating on the eggs, he said, "Ninety-nine percent of the time, there's no one here but me and Big Blue. Conversation is something I'm not use to."

"Who is Big Blue?"

"My dog. I left him in the barn with the other animals. I thought you might be frightened of him."

Everleigh put her hands on her waist. "You have a dog and didn't tell me?"

Turning the eggs, he reached into the cabinet for plates. "Yes. I didn't tell you about the chickens or the pigs either. Do you like chickens? What do you think of pigs?"

The man could definitely be annoying.

"Eh, they're okay. But I've always wanted a dog. Mother said I couldn't have one because she would have to take care of it," she said softly. At the thought of her mother, her chest ached and she wondered if the pain would ever go away. She would never stop missing her family, but when would a memory come without torment? When did the heartache get easier to bear?

"When I go into town, I leave him in the barn," he said, sliding the eggs onto the plates and handing her one.

They sat at the small table.

"Is he a big dog?"

"He's about fifty pounds and six hands high."

"That's a big dog," she said, cutting her eggs with her fork and knife.

He stopped eating and watched her. "Why are you massacring your eggs?"

"What do you mean?"

"You're slicing them into little pieces. Can't you do that with your fork?"

She tilted her head and gave him a haughty look. "This was how I was raised. My dad always cut his eggs this way. Who taught you how to daintily eat your eggs?"

"My mother."

"Well, my father taught me. And he was from New York."

"My mother was the daughter of a preacher. So la-ti-da."

It was the longest discussion they'd had and it was over how to cut eggs.

They finished their breakfast in silence. Christmas was fewer than two weeks away and memories of past holidays haunted her. Closing her eyes, she fought the pain the word *mother* invoked.

"You all right?"

Opening her eyes, she stared across the table at him. "I'm fine. Just dreading Christmas." She propped her chin in her hand and stared at him. "Where are your folks?"

"In The Dalles, Oregon."

He got up from the table and put water on the stove to heat. "Don't you miss them?"

"Every day. Mother writes me a letter about once a month and occasionally she'll send me cookies," he said, his voice wistful. "But I like owning my own spread and I wouldn't go back unless it was to visit."

"Must be hard living out here all alone."

"Nah," he said. "I've gotten used to it." He turned and stared at her. "It's why I don't talk much."

She shook her head at him. "You should get into town more."

"I go when I need to," he said, effectively cutting her off. The man was difficult to have a conversation with. But then again, her father hadn't been the talker. That was her mother.

"Do you want me to help with those dishes?" she asked, watching him and thinking she'd never seen her father do dishes. Her mother had been in charge of the home and the kitchen had been her domain. This was unusual, different, and she kind of liked watching him.

The man wore a pair of jeans like she'd never seen. They defined the muscles in his legs and his backside, which was well-shaped and cute. She'd never noticed a man's backside before, but with his back turned to her while his hands were in soapy water, she was enjoying the view. Didn't hurt to look as long as he didn't catch her.

Suddenly he turned around and frowned.

"Uh, what do you want me to do?" she asked, knowing she'd been caught.

"Why don't you throw another log on the fire," he said. "I'm finishing these dishes and then going to the barn to check on the animals."

"Didn't you do that already this morning?"

"Yes."

"They need feeding again?"

"No, I want to make certain they have enough water and feed and they're staying warm," he replied not looking at her.

Why did she get the feeling he was going out to the barn to escape being with her? Why did it seem he wanted to put distance between them?

She watched as he pulled on his coat, then boots, and finally his hat and scarf. Opening the door, he stepped into the blizzard. She ran to the window in the kitchen above the sink and watched him disappear into the swirling snowflakes. She could see the rope near the house moving.

She could walk to the barn in the snow. She wanted to see his animals. She wanted to see his dog. She wanted out of this darn building for just a few moments. Sure, she could pick up her knitting or even read a book she'd brought, but more than anything she wanted to escape this tension filled room.

Right now, her life felt out of control and the feel of a sweet dog licking her hand would be something she hadn't experienced since she was a child. Running into the bedroom, she found his clothes and put them on. The pants were way too long and she rolled the hem up and stuffed the material into her boots. She took a scarf and slid it through the belt loops. Yesterday, several times, she'd come dangerously close to losing her pants and embarrassing herself even more in front of Seth. She couldn't manage the snow, the rope, and the pants, so she tied the scarf around her waist.

Slipping her coat on, she took a deep breath and decided to brave the cold.

Opening the door, the blast of frigid air almost had her turning back. She wanted to see the dog. Snowflakes poured from the sky, blinding her. Groping in the snow for the rope she knew he'd tied to the house, relief filled her when she found the lifeline. Stepping off the snow covered porch, she was unprepared when she sank to mid-thigh in a drift. Her dress would never have made it through the mounds.

As it was, she followed the path that Seth had made to the barn. A gust of wind almost blew her over, but she hung tightly to the rope. The snow was falling so thickly, she couldn't see anything but whiteness surrounding her and the cold seeped through the pants to her legs leaving her skin chilled to the bone. Her hands began to numb and she feared she would drop the rope and never find it again in the snow.

This had been a crazy idea. Though she barely knew Seth, she knew enough about him to know he wasn't going to be happy. He would be angry that she'd left the safety of the house. All because she wanted to see a dog. Sometimes she did silly things without thinking through the consequences.

She could hear her mother's voice inside her head telling her to think before she acted and still she'd forgotten and found herself in trouble. Right now, she just wanted to reach that barn door at the end of this rope and slip inside where hopefully it was warmer. And she could pet his dog.

When she was about to lose hope and feeling in her fingers, she felt a handle in front of her. She opened the door and walked inside.

"What are you doing here?" he demanded, staring at her, his eyes darkening.

Shaking, her lips frozen, she tried to talk. "I...was...bored. I...thought...I'd...come...see...your....dog."

He grabbed her by the arm and pulled her toward a small stove. Seizing her hand, he began to rub her fingers gently between his hands. "If you'd dropped that rope, you could have wandered off and I would never have found you. Don't you ever go out of the house in weather like this again without me by your side. Do you understand me?"

"Yes," she said, shivering so hard, she feared her bones would break. "I didn't think it would be this bad. It's scary out there."

"You could have died," he said, his face taut with rage. "You're soaking wet, you're freezing and..."

He gazed down into her face. They were mere inches apart. He pulled her against him, the solid strength of his body crashed into her and she gasped as she felt every hard inch of him through the pants she wore. Her body thrummed with a sudden awakening, The smell of him flooded her and she gasped as a thousand needles stung her hands, but he didn't let her go. Staring into her eyes, he gazed at her lips and her nerves seemed to awaken and stretch to a tightness she'd never experienced before.

"Ah, hell," he said as his lips slammed down on hers.

CHAPTER 7

Seth knew he wasn't being gentle. This woman had been driving him crazy for two days with her sweet lips and her luscious curves and the way her eyes would glance at him half-lidded as if she were peeking out beneath those long lashes. Crushing her mouth beneath his, her taste flooded his senses and he longed to pick her up and carry her to the hayloft and unwrap her like a Christmas present. His hand reached up to caress the side of her cheek, holding her mouth firmly in place.

A moan escaped the back of her throat and slowly his rational mind overcame his desire. Abruptly, he stepped away, putting distance between them, knowing where those kinds of kisses led and the results.

Breathing hard, his chest rising and falling as he stared at her in shock, as he tried to gather himself when all he wanted to do was continue.

"I'll take you back," he said.

Standing in front of him, her hand had gone to her mouth, and she gazed at him in wonder. "Who taught you to kiss like that?"

He laughed. "That's not open for discussion. Now, let's go."

"No," she responded, glaring at him like she was just stubborn enough to resist.

All he wanted was some time away from her. Some time to get his desire back under control. Some time to clear his head of the way she looked in those skintight, soaking wet pants, and the way she smelled so sweetly of roses and lavender. Of the way she seem to engulf his little home, making the room feel so tight and small with her there at his every move. He just needed some time to regain control. Now she had invaded his sanctuary and refused to leave.

"Only if I can take the dog with me," she said, her hand stroking Big Blue, the traitor staring up at her with adoring eyes.

"All right," he said, thinking that would mean letting the dog out every few hours. But maybe that would be good, because that would give him time to quench this physical hunger that consumed him. Even with Catherine, he'd never been so captivated with the urge to take her to bed.

Maybe because he knew everyone would assume he and Everleigh had done the deed while he was trying to be the honorable man and not let his passions rule him. But being noble and ethical was damn hard. Especially with a woman as beautiful as Everleigh.

"Let's go," he said. When they reached the door, he laid his hand on her arm. "Wait."

Quickly, he slid a rope from around his waist and tied it to her belt and then hooked her onto the line. She gazed down at the setup. "Really, you think this is necessary?"

"I'm not taking any chances. If something happens, then I'll be the one lost between here and the house, not you."

Frowning, she bit her lip, tilted her head and gazed at him. "And you think that would be a good thing for me? This girl from New York City has no clue on how to survive in this kind of weather."

"You'd learn."

"Promise me, you won't let that happen," she said softly. "I don't want your death on my conscience."

The way she was looking at him had him rethinking leaving the barn. But if they didn't, his animals were going to hear and see things they'd never witnessed before. The snow had to cool him down.

"I'm not ready to die just yet," he said, his mind imagining the two of them naked, their limbs intertwined.

Opening the barn door, they looked out at the blowing snow and the dog whined.

"How long can this last?" she asked.

"The last really big storm blew for three days and took me almost a week to dig out."

"Wait, Big Blue," he told the dog and walked over and grabbed a leash. Quickly, he secured the dog. He knew he would stay beside him, but he feared Big Blue getting too far away and getting lost in the blinding snow.

Holding onto the dog, with Everleigh walking in front of him, they made their way from the barn. The deep snow came up to the dog's chest, creating a trough wherever he walked.

Halfway there, he watched in disbelief as Everleigh slipped on something in the snow, her feet flying up in the air as she came down hard in the drift, tripping him.

He landed on top of her. Even in the cold, he could feel her soft curves and warm body. Her breasts were crushed beneath his chest. She glanced up into his eyes and laughed.

"Why is this so difficult? Why does it seem like everything improper keeps happening to me?"

What could he say? She'd done nothing wrong and yet they were starting that descent into dangerous territory. One where he'd find a shotgun and a preacher waiting for him at the end.

Hanging onto the rope, Seth felt the tautness suddenly go slack and knew immediately the line had broken.

A gust of ice and snow battered them and he watched the end

of the rope flapping in the breeze, flakes of snow hurtling at them so fast, he felt like he was drowning.

"Are you all right?" he yelled into the wind, rolling off her and standing. For once, he had to agree with her. This wasn't helping him keep his distance.

Everleigh sat up. "I hate this."

He reached down and helped her to her feet. She glanced down at the empty hook. "I broke the rope."

"Yes," he replied, wondering if it was worth trying to find the other end that the wind had blown. "Stay right here. Don't move. I'm going to try to find the end of the rope."

"But..."

"And hold onto the dog's leash," he said, handing it to her.

The dog barked in protest as Seth walked away searching for the frayed ends of the rope leading to the house. Afraid to walk too far, he made a circle. Minutes later, he gave up. As he retraced his own footsteps, he heard her singing.

"Where are you, Seth Ketchum. Where did you go? Come back to me and don't leave me in the snow."

A grin spread across his face. The woman had certainly made his life entertaining, never letting it get boring. It was a unique way for her to reach out to him and it warmed his heart, but not his toes. They had to keep walking and hope they made it to the house.

When he reached her, Big Blue started barking, his tail wagging. "I heard you singing."

"Good, I was so afraid you would get lost. Did you find the rope?" she yelled over the blowing wind and snow.

"No. Clip your hook into the back of my pants. We're going to try to make it without the rope. It's all we can do."

She closed her eyes for a moment.

"What are you doing? Let's go."

"Praying. Don't interrupt me."

How could he argue with her about reaching out to help from above. They were going to need all the help they could get.

Opening her eyes, she stepped behind him and he felt the hook.

"Now give me the leash," he said.

"I want to keep him."

"Give me the dog," he demanded.

"All right," she said, frustrated as she handed him the leash.

Seth leaned down and rubbed the dogs head. "Big Blue take us home."

The dog whined and then began to plow through the snow. What seemed like hours, but was only minutes later, Seth could see the front door and heaved a sigh of relief. Now he would have to tie a new rope to the barn, but at least he knew he could find his way back.

"Good job, Blue."

Stepping into the warmth of the house, he took a moment to savor the heat. "I have to go back out and string the rope again."

"No, don't go," she said. "It makes me nervous. I'm scared something will happen to you."

He glanced at her, surprised. No one ever worried about him anymore. No one expressed any concern that he could get hurt. And yet, he had to do this. Sometime later today, he'd have to go back out to the barn and take care of the animals.

Reaching out, he touched her on the arm. "I'll be fine. I'll be back in after a bit. Why don't you have a nice hot cup of coffee waiting for me."

She grabbed him, pulling him to her and kissed him solidly on the lips. A wave of desire, raced through him, her scent intoxicating and warming him. He didn't want to leave, but stay here in her arms.

Releasing Seth, she stepped back. "That's to make certain you'll come back."

Staring in shock, he smiled. Was that a promise? Should he even go down that road?

This was turning out to be quite a day. A day he didn't know if spending time outside would cool the temperature rising inside him.

CHAPTER 8

*T*he next morning when she opened her eyes, she knew immediately. Her head pounded, nausea roiled her stomach, and the telltale signs of cramping gripped her. Could her timing be any worse?

Lying in bed, tears welled up and spilled down her cheeks of their own accord. Well, just great, *Aunt Flo's* timing topped off a spectacularly bad week. She felt lousy. She was stuck in a cabin with a man who intrigued her, her reputation was in the outhouse, and now this. Of all the embarrassing things to happen while they were together.

It was bad enough they shared the same slop jar, but the weather made it impossible to go outside to the outhouse and he only had one jar. What were they supposed to do? She was so ready for this to end.

Rising from the bed, she dressed and then laid back down. She just wanted to stay here in this room, but it was late.

A knock sounded on the door. "Everleigh, breakfast is ready."

"Coming," she called.

With a sigh, she wiped the tears from her eyes and slowly

rose. Life certainly had a way of humbling her. Nothing could be worse than coming home to discover your family home destroyed and your parents dead. And now a trip she'd been anticipating, wanting to spend time with her remaining family, had turned disastrous. First, the snow storm and now Aunt Flo.

Standing, she went into the kitchen.

"Good morning," Seth said, gazing at her, his eyes narrowing as he seemed to study her.

"Morning," she said and sank down onto a chair. A cramp had her almost doubling over, but she bit her lip and sat quietly absorbing the pain.

"Are you all right?" he asked. "You look a little peaked this morning."

"Fine," she said, not wanting to discuss with him that the curse of being a woman was upon her. Not exactly table conversation.

He sat a plate of eggs in front of her and the smell of the fried eggs engulfed her. Gagging, she rose from the table.

"Excuse me," she said and hurried into the bedroom, where she lay on the bed.

The chill in the room had her shivering and she soon climbed beneath the heavy quilts. Lying there, she wanted to die.

Ten minutes later, there was a knock on the door.

"Yes," she asked, not wanting him to see her this way. Not wanting to explain.

"Can I come in?" he asked.

"Yes," she said.

He opened the door and carried a tray. Frowning, she watched him approach the side of the bed.

"I thought you might need this," he said and handed her a bed warmer. "My mother said it always made her feel better."

She glanced up at him, her eyes filling with tears. He knew and was trying to make her feel better. His kindness filled her with warmth and gratitude, and made her uncomfortable at the same time. "Thank you."

"I also brought you a hot toddy. It's a little early in the morning, but it might help you sleep for a while," he said quietly. He cleared his throat and looked out the window and then back at her. "I also brought you some rags. I didn't know if you would need them or not."

Stunned, she stared at him. "How did you know?"

He laughed. "I have three sisters and a mother. For my own wellbeing, I learned to recognize the signs."

She smiled and took the hot beverage. "Thank you for being so nice to me."

"You're welcome."

"So does this mean you don't dislike me anymore?"

Chuckling he smiled. "When I realized you reminded me of Catherine, my previous fiancé, I understood why I reacted the way I did. So no, I don't dislike you and to be honest, you're really not like her at all. You have more spunk, more stamina, and you're tough in a good way."

Sipping the warm liquid she nodded. "I don't dislike you either."

"I kind of gathered that when you kissed me yesterday."

"That was just a good luck kiss."

The memory of the kisses they'd shared the day before left her breathless. The way his lips had claimed hers, his tongue stroking her mouth, the warmth that had gripped her middle like a raging firestorm.

"If you disliked me, you wouldn't have done it," he said, gazing at her like he wanted to lean down and kiss her again. And she wanted him to, but knew this was not the time nor the place.

"No, I wouldn't have. And I was scared," she said, staring at his lips, wishing she could taste them again. Before things got out of hand, she needed to get to her uncle's. It was past time. "So I guess this means we're not going to my uncle's again today."

"Still snowing. Though it seems to be slowing some."

"Do you think we'll be able to leave tomorrow?"

Right now, there was an awareness of each other between them. She felt like they were circling one another, dancing around the tension that drew her to him. She had to make it to her uncle's or fear that whatever this thing between them was would soon explode and consume her.

"Hard to say. Even after it stops snowing, travel is going to be near impossible for a while."

Tears filled her eyes and she wanted to scream, but knew it was nothing more than the curse. Long ago, she'd recognized when Aunt Flo visited, her emotions seem to erupt. "I can't stay here until spring."

"I promise you, the first day I think it's safe to leave, we'll load up the sleigh and be on our way. I give you my word."

She gazed at him, and the strength and conviction in his voice made her realize he was being honest with her. He would do what he said. "All right."

"Now, finish your hot toddy and get some rest."

Nodding, she handed him the empty cup and yawned. "I think I'll curl up here with the bed warmer and rest for a while."

"That sounds like a good idea. I'll be right out here if you need me. See you later," he said.

"Seth," she called when he reached the door.

"Yes?"

"Thanks for taking care of me."

And she meant it. She realized he had watched over her and kept her safe during the worst snow storm she'd ever experienced. No one other than her parents had ever cared for her. Some lucky woman would be fortunate to have him as her husband.

"You're welcome."

He walked out the door and she snuggled deeper into the covers. Why couldn't she find a man like him in New York?

If she could find someone like Seth, she'd marry him in a

minute. Instead, she seemed to find men who were boring and wanted her to become their social hostess. And she was done with that type of man. Give her a rugged man who knew how to take care of his woman. That's what she wanted. One that was not frightened by her insistence of having a career.

CHAPTER 9

*L*ate that afternoon, Seth was surprised and pleased to see Everleigh emerge from the bedroom. There was more color in her cheeks and she didn't have that haggard look in her eyes any longer.

"Feeling better?" he asked, standing in the small kitchen stirring a bubbling pot.

"Yes," she said, and made her way to the lumpy sofa he'd purchased at a second hand store.

"I thought we'd have some venison chili tonight for supper; is that okay?" he asked, uncertain she would like deer meat.

"Of course. What can I do to help?"

He wasn't going to let her work in the kitchen after feeling poorly this morning. She could sit and watch him, and besides, this kept her at a safe distance.

While she was sleeping, he'd made the decision to try to make it to her uncle's tomorrow no matter what. Between yesterday's kisses and then today when she'd glanced up at him with those big emerald eyes brimming with tears of gratitude, he'd known he had to get her out of here. She was a danger to his bachelorhood. And while he eventually wanted to marry and have children, being forced to wed someone was not the way he wanted to acquire a wife.

It wasn't the story he wanted to tell his children when they asked how they'd met. And yet, his own parents had pretended they were man and wife as they made their way to Oregon. But theirs was a story of adventure and love. Not of being holed up during a blizzard.

He glanced at her from the kitchen. "You relax. Tonight, I'm taking care of dinner."

"Are you sure?" she asked. "I'm feeling better."

"It's no big deal. I'm use to cooking for myself."

Funny how he'd never planned on living alone, and yet, here was a single man. He'd never planned on leaving The Dalles until Catherine had made it impossible to continue living there.

While he prepared cornbread to go with their chili, she sat staring out the window. "It doesn't seem to be snowing as hard."

"It's not."

Staring out at the white landscape that was as far as she could see, she turned back to him. "Are those mountains in the distance?"

"Yes, you haven't been able to see them because of the blizzard. But it seems to be letting up and tomorrow, after I feed the cattle, if the snow is not too deep, we'll try to make it to your uncle's. I'm sure you're ready to get there."

He watched as her eyes widened and she smiled. "Great! I can't wait to see them. Christmas is soon and after the first of the year, I'll be heading back to New York City."

Seth felt a pang of pain near his heart. What was the matter with him? At first, he hadn't even liked her, but now, well, she was growing on him and the thought of being so far away left him sad. She had a life there, a big time career working for some fancy newspaper. The memory of kissing her in the barn returned like a slap to the gut and he quickly focused on pouring the cornmeal mixture into a pan. That kiss was better than any he'd ever experienced before. Better than even Catherine's kisses.

"Tell me about your job in New York City."

She glanced at him working in the kitchen, her green eyes dark with mystery, not excited like he'd expected her to be when she spoke of her big career.

"When I graduated college, I wanted to be a journalist with the largest newspaper in America. And that's where I'll be starting to work in January when I get home."

Something about her story seemed too perfect, too exact, and she didn't seem excited that she would be writing and reporting for a world-renowned paper. But then again, he'd never read the newspaper. Occasionally, he'd pick up the local paper in town when he was looking for new livestock or needed something in the want ads.

"What will you write about? Current affairs or an article for ladies?" he asked, curious about what she would be covering for the paper. He hadn't gone to college, but a friend of his had covered the farm news for an Oregon paper and he'd often wondered how he came up with what to write about.

"I don't know," she said evading his question. "They haven't told me."

Twisting her hands in her lap, she glanced out the window again. "What about you? How did you get to be a rancher?"

Sighing, he put the cornbread into the oven and then sat across from her in a rocker he'd made himself. It had been a project to keep him occupied two winters ago so he wouldn't concentrate on feeling so alone. Maybe after Everleigh left, he would talk to James, her uncle, about who in town he could court. Maybe it was time he tried to find love once again.

"I had been courting a girl for over six months and asked her to marry me," he said quietly. "My parents had a ranch just outside of The Dalles, Oregon, where I'd grown up. I'd gone to school, church there, and this girl was a member of our community. Everyone said we were going to be so happy. A week before the wedding, she expressed some doubts, but I just thought she was nervous. We were attending big parties, family gatherings and bridal showers, so we were both overwhelmed with the wedding."

Leaning his head back against the rocker, he took a deep breath and released it slowly. He hated talking about this time of his life and didn't even understand why he was telling Everleigh.

"The day of the wedding arrived and I was so excited. We would start our life together. My parents had given us ten acres to build a house on their spread. I woke up feeling like it was going to be the best day of my life," he said with a chuckle. "All the people we knew were seated in the church. I walked out the door to stand beside the preacher."

He hesitated, hating what he would say next, remembering the nerves that had gripped him, but the excitement as well. "We were all waiting for her to come down the aisle. But she never showed. Her father finally came and told me she was missing. He couldn't find her."

Her eyes grew wide. "What happened to her?"

"She eloped with a man she'd only known a week. A man she'd met while volunteering at the school. The worst part was she didn't cancel the wedding or let me know. She embarrassed me in front of the whole town."

Seth ran his hand through his hair, leaning back in the rocker, he moved the chair with his legs. When he'd left Oregon, he'd sworn never to talk about Catherine again, but here he was, telling Everleigh about the most humiliating day of his life. He'd loved Catherine, but time and distance had made him realize the break-up was for the best.

"That must have been terrible."

"The whole town pitied me. When people looked my way, they remembered me as that poor boy Catherine left standing at the altar. I was no longer Seth Ketchum, Rachel and Wade Ketchum's son. I was that young man jilted by Catherine."

She stared at him, her face reflecting exactly how the people in town had treated him. But this time it didn't bother him.

"What did you do?"

"After two months, I had to leave or go crazy. My father had given me two horses as a wedding gift and I packed my saddle bags and headed for South Dakota. But then I came across this property for sale by an old man who could no longer take care of it and bought the land and house from him. I've been here ever since."

Sitting with her feet tucked up underneath the skirts she wore, her hair loose about her shoulders, her dark emerald eyes gazing at him with empathy and kindness, she was beautiful and she was dangerous. Her womanly scent mixed with roses and lavender reached him across the room and he stared at her full lips so rich and inviting that he wanted to taste them again, but knew that was not a good idea.

"She was a fool," Everleigh said suddenly, her voice a breathless rush. "To give up a man like you for someone she'd just met. I bet she's regretting her decision at this very moment."

He shrugged. "Don't know and don't care. I've put her in the past and moved on."

It was true. He had moved on, but he hadn't searched for anyone else. Maybe it was time. Before he fell for someone he knew he couldn't have. He stared at Everleigh.

"So why haven't you found someone else?"

"I've been busy. That first year, I had to rebuild the barn, stock it with hay and get prepared for the winter. Slowly I've been building my herd and trying to fix up the place. You're the first woman who's been here."

Silence filled the room as she stared down at her hands. Then she looked up at him. "Are you ever going to marry?"

Of course, he was, but he wasn't a man who jumped into

something without knowing what he was getting. But he also wasn't a man who was easy to get to know. And yet with Everleigh, it hadn't been hard. Sure, at first, they'd butted heads, but they'd also been facing a life-threatening situation, which had put them both under a lot of stress.

"Someday, when I find the right woman," he said, gazing at her, wishing for just a moment that they had a chance. How had he gone from complete dislike to suddenly wishing he could take her in his arms and express his growing feelings. But she was different from Catherine. She wasn't the girl he'd assumed she was when she got off that train. No, she was better. "I want a family."

"Me, too," she said. "I didn't realize how much I wanted children until my own family was killed. But now, I'd like to have a husband and children of my own."

The sound of the bubbling chili splashing on the stove had him jumping up and running into the kitchen. Why did it seem they were both yearning for the same things except she wanted hers over two thousand miles away with her career.

Somehow, he had to forget all about Everleigh and get her to her uncle's as soon as possible, before his heart was broken once again.

CHAPTER 10

*T*wo days later, after supper, Everleigh felt the need to get up and help Seth. Aunt Flo had come and gone and she was back to normal. It wasn't like this didn't happen on a regular basis and next time, she would remember the hot toddy. Unfortunately, the snow had continued to fall, though not quite as hard. Sooner or later, it had to stop. It just had to as every day spent with Seth sealed her fate.

"You don't have to help me," he said. "Go, sit down."

Glancing at him, she stared into his dark blue eyes and full lips, remembering how it felt when he'd smashed her against his chest and kissed her senseless. Why did she long for that again? "I have to do something. I think I'm getting cabin fever. I just can't sit here anymore."

He smiled. "Understand. Then you can wash and I'll dry."

"That works."

He poured the hot water into a big dishpan and added soap. Handing her a rag, she started with their silverware. "I can't believe you cook and clean for yourself."

"Who else is going to do it? It's not like I can hire a maid, and no woman is going to live out here without a ring on her finger."

The thought of another woman in the cabin filled her with jealousy, which was ridiculous. Tomorrow, she'd go to her uncle's and they could hopefully pretend nothing happened and soon she'd return to New York and he'd be here in Mistletoe.

Chuckling, she turned to him. "I guess not. Very practical, Seth."

"That's what my mother used to say to me. I was the practical one of her children."

How lucky he was to have brothers and sisters. She'd never thought being an only child was bad until the death of her parents when there had been no one to share the grief with. No one to talk about the good times. Sure, she had friends in New York, but no family. Not even an aunt or uncle.

"How many brothers and sisters do you have?"

"There are the three orphans Toby, Grace, and Daniel who are just like blood brothers and sisters. Then I came along next, then there was Sarah, Mary, Walker, and Joseph. Eight children all growing up together. Our house was quite a circus, but we were surrounded by love."

The thought of a home filled with eight children was something she couldn't even comprehend. But it sounded fun.

"Wasn't it hard to go off and leave them all behind?"

"It's the hardest thing I've ever done. I miss them and my parents, who are getting up in years."

"You're so lucky. I don't have any brothers and sisters. In fact, I was born late in my parents' life. They had been married fifteen years when suddenly I came along." Sometimes she wondered if she wanted to return to New York just because that's where her roots were. That's where memories had been made and she felt obligated to return there. Yet, it was also where her career would begin.

"I hope to go see them sometime soon."

"Who will take care of your ranch? You can't go off and leave the animals alone," she asked.

"I've grown enough that I hope to hire some hands next year. Right now, your uncle is kind enough to help me out, but after my bull gored him, I doubt he's going to be available again."

"It was your bull that hurt my uncle?"

For her uncle to come help Seth, he had to be close to Seth's ranch. So close, but yet so cold and snowy and far away.

"Yes, the bull has his own pasture, but he likes to come a calling on my heifers."

She started laughing, the idea of a bull making a call on a lady cow, ridiculous. "Of course, that was before all the snow."

"Yes," he said quietly.

She reached around him to wipe off the table and bumped against him, her breasts brushed against his arm, sending a delicious tingle zipping along her spine straight to her groin. She gave a little gasp and glanced at him to see if he noticed. His eyes darkened and his lips squeezed together tightly drawing his cheekbones taut.

Since the day he kissed her, there seemed to be this awareness coursing between them that had her on edge, trying to avoid his touch, his smell, the very memory of his kiss.

Seth was a rancher. She was a suffragette, a long way from home, from her friends. Yet she wanted to explore those full luscious lips of his and see if she'd react the same way or was it just a coincidence that when he was near, she'd almost gone up in flames.

He moved closer to the cabinet to avoid her and she quickly wiped down the table. Turning back, he stepped backward and bumped into her chest, almost knocking her down. He grabbed her arm to keep her from falling. This kitchen was so small, two people could barely maneuver.

"Excuse me," he said, gazing into her eyes.

His fingers still gripped her by the arm as they stared at one another. He licked his lips and then he was crushing her against him, his mouth covering hers, sealing them together, taking her like a raging storm. Demanding, crushing, and yet tender at the same time. He kissed her like she'd never been kissed, sliding his tongue along her lips, tormenting her, making her ache with need.

Cradled against his pelvis, she could feel the rigid hardness of him and was shocked at the wantonness. Yet a part of her also wanted to push toward that male hard flesh that seemed so intriguing. Moaning a rough, brusque sound, he deepened the kiss until she thought she would faint. His strong, tanned hands gripped her head and held her lips captive as he plundered her mouth.

Suddenly, he stopped, his breathing harsh, his eyes glazed as he looked at her, his swollen manhood still firmly planted between her thighs.

"I've got to get out of here," he gasped.

Releasing her, he stepped away putting distance between them. Distance she didn't want. She wanted to continue what he'd started. She wanted to feel what happened next. She wanted Seth in a way she'd never imagined wanting a man.

Grabbing his coat, he yanked it on. "Don't come looking for me. I'll be out in the barn until late."

Shoving his hat on his head, he walked to the door and then glanced back at her. "Goodnight."

Standing there with the dish rag still in her hand, she watched him walk out the door, feeling stunned at what had just happened. Sure, he'd kissed her before, but this time it had been different. It had been intimate and left her confused and frustrated and angry.

She threw the rag at the door. Why had he stopped?

CHAPTER 11

*T*he next morning, Seth tromped through the snow to the barn and swung open the door. The bone-numbing cold settled in around him as he pushed the sled out of the barn. Tiny flakes of snow still fell in the dawn light, but they may have been from the light breeze that stirred the drifts.

He had to get Everleigh to her uncle's. She couldn't stay here a moment longer or he feared the ramifications of them being together. The attraction between them was getting out of control and he didn't know how much longer he'd be able to keep his hands to himself. And then there were the consequences of them being alone. She'd been here almost a week. Time was running out on them and he had to get her to James's house or be forced to marry her.

Pulling the sleigh out of the barn into the early morning sunshine, he went back for the horses. Several minutes later, he had them all hooked up and ready to go.

Going into the house, he knocked on her bedroom door. It was still early, but after last night, he wanted to get on the road as soon as possible. They were less than an hour away and it was time. This attraction, like a small keg of dynamite, was just a short fuse from going off, damaging them both.

"It's early," she called through the door, her voice groggy. His mind pictured Everleigh in her night clothes, her hair tousled, her gaze sleepy, and for a moment, he wanted to open the door and climb in that warm bed. His insides twisted into a hard knot of desire. Thoughts like this were the very reason she had to leave.

"The sleigh is ready. I'm taking you to your uncle's this morning," he called, wishing she would hurry before temptation overwhelmed the sensible, rational part of his anatomy. With the snow piled deep, it would take them longer to reach her uncle's. For his own sanity, he had to get her out of his here.

"I'll be right out," she said, sounding more alert.

Ten minutes later, she rushed out of the room, breathless, beautiful, and damn tempting. "I didn't know we were leaving this morning."

"The weather looks decent and I thought we should try," he said, putting as much distance between them as he could. Just gazing at her full lips and remembering how they tasted was a distraction he didn't need. "Christmas is a week away. You should spend as much time as possible with your family."

And let him recover from her nearness.

Grabbing her coat, she slipped it over her dress. "My trunk is already packed. I'm ready."

For a moment, he felt a pang of disappointment clench his chest and he wondered at the sensation. The stinging, burning ache was from the realization that he'd miss her feminine presence awakening the man inside him. Why did it seem she was eager to leave, when the masculine part of him wanted her to stay while the logical part said she had to go. Dealing with her had him all torn up inside, knowing what he should do and knowing what he wanted to do and none of it the right thing.

And Seth's mother had instilled in him that a good man was always conscientious, principled, and responsible.

Right now, he wanted to cast aside the disciplined part of him and let the virile man in him react to the soft, tempting woman in front of him. They had to go, now.

He carried her trunk out to the sleigh, the cold wind a welcome respite, and then turned to help her into the sleigh. Placing his hands around her waist, he lifted her into the vehicle, breathing in the scent of roses, causing his breath to quicken. She glanced down at him and smiled. The smile had his loins tightening. He'd miss her nearness, the smell of her filling his home and the silly grin that tugged something in his chest.

"Thank you."

"You're welcome," he said and tucked the heavy pelt over her feet and legs. "Next stop, Uncle James's place."

The sun was shining brightly off the snow as the horse pulled the sleigh up the drive to the road. Seth had to focus on the road and not on the woman sitting next to him. But that was difficult.

"I can't wait to see them," she said, her breath frosty in the morning air.

"I'm sure they've been worried about you," he replied, noticing how the wind was starting to blow, sending ice crystals stinging his face.

"Oh," she said, ducking her head to avoid the stinging flakes. "That wind is bitter cold."

As they pulled out onto the road, away from the pine trees that lined his property, it was then he saw the dark blue cloud off in the distance. Maybe it was just an illusion. Maybe it was not what he feared. Maybe he was tempting fate. He'd keep his eye on that ominous cloud and hope they would arrive before the storm. Or hope the cloud disappeared, but he urged the horses a little faster.

Quietly, he held the reins, watching the birds, knowing his instincts were warning him, but not wanting to pay attention.

Fifteen minutes later, the sun disappeared behind the racing clouds and the first sprinkles of snow began to fall.

"Not again," he said, beneath his breath as he pulled the horse to a stop. With the deep snow, it would take them another hour to reach her uncle's and he didn't think they had that much time.

She turned and glanced at him, her eyes big and questioning. "Why are you stopping? What's wrong?"

"Can't you see? Another storm is almost upon us."

She shook her head. "No," she cried. "Don't stop. Keep going. We can make it to my uncle's. We're not that far."

"I'm not willing to take the chance. In another few moments, the snow is going to start falling faster and thicker. I won't be able to see. We could get lost so easily and I'm not willing to risk our lives. We're turning back," he said, frustration gripping his chest.

Another night with her in the house. Another chance of the two of them being overcome by temptation. Another couple of days with no chaperone.

No one would believe them if they said nothing happened. No one would care. Seth was an honorable man and he was determined to protect Everleigh from gossip.

Turning the sleigh in the middle of the road, she threw off the pelt and hopped out, sinking in the drifts. "I'm not going back with you. I'll walk."

He stopped the vehicle. "What are you doing?"

"I'm walking to my uncle's," she said, tromping in the snow. It came past her knees and he watched her battling the snow for a few moments, taking another step. Struggling through the drifts, she would never make it. He knew she wouldn't, but he had to let her reach that conclusion. So he sat patiently waiting, wishing she'd hurry since they were running out of time.

She took three more steps and then put her hands to her face.

"Get in the sleigh," he said softly.

"I want to go to my uncle's," she cried.

"I'll take you just as soon as we get a break in this weather," he promised her. "When I think it's safe, we'll try again. I tried, but another storm is about to hit us."

Just then the wind howled as the flakes flew faster. Struggling against the wind, she made it back to the sleigh and crawled in. Quickly, he wrapped the pelt over her feet and legs feeling her body shivering next to him. With a snap of the reins, he called out to the horses and with a jolt, the sleigh started the short journey back to the house.

By the time they reached the barn, the storm's fury was just starting to unleash. Hopping out of the sleigh, he quickly connected the rope between the house and barn. Then he turned to help Everleigh out of the sleigh.

When they reached the door, she ran into the bedroom sobbing, slamming the door behind her.

With a sigh, he let her go and then went into the weather to care for the horses. Well, that certainly hadn't worked out the way he'd hoped.

Yet, part of him was glad she was still here, and that part scared him worse than the storm unleashing outside the barn. All he could think about was the softness of her body, the taste of her lips, and the feel of her in his arms.

CHAPTER 12

*E*verleigh lay on the bed, listening to the wind howl outside, rattling the glass panes. She was beginning to worry she would never get out of this house. And even if she did, would her uncle demand they marry? She glanced around the bedroom and wondered what it would be like to be married to Seth. He was handsome, could kiss like the devil, and seemed like a gentle man.

After their explosive embrace the other night, she'd not seen him until this morning when he'd told her he was taking her to her uncle's. Now disappointment raged inside her like the storm outside. She'd wanted to leave, to escape the feelings he evoked.

She liked Seth. She knew they were in a difficult place and if her father had been alive, he would have already demanded Seth marry her. But was that what she wanted?

Like every young woman, she'd always dreamed that when she married, it would be because she loved the man, not because they were forced into marriage. Not because some blizzard had trapped them together. Even though she knew nothing had happened between them, she realized it wouldn't take many more kisses before she would beg him to show her this mysterious act between a man and a woman. Her mother had only given her a few sketchy details and her friends in college had whispered about lovemaking, but never professed to actually have experienced a man.

And now a mammoth snowstorm had her locked inside Seth's home for days, and everyone would assume they'd done the deed.

"Merry Christmas to you too," she said aloud.

Sighing, she sat up, wiped her face, straightened her hair and stepped into the living area. Though their apartment in New York had not been much bigger than this doll house, it had an extra bedroom and a water closet where there was running water. Not in Seth's home.

Here, they were in the wilderness and while she loved the snow and the pine trees and the beautiful scenery, it was so quiet compared to the bustling city she'd left. It was so quiet, sometimes the sound of her own heartbeat could be heard in the room.

The front door opened and Seth came in, carrying her trunk.

Shaking her head, she hurried over to hold the door. "Thank you."

Gazing at him, she realized she had acted selfishly, but part of her knew it was her last chance to save her reputation or face the consequences. "Look at you, you're covered in snow. You're wet. You need to change out of those wet clothes right away."

He stared, his blue eyes gazing at her in a way that made her heart race a little faster as he removed his hat, coat, and his big hands from his gloves. "Haven't we gone through this before?"

She gave a little laugh. "Yes."

Licking her lips, she quickly glanced away, a shiver twisting her nerves lowdown as she imagined the feel of those hands touching the intimate parts of her body. "I'll fix lunch while you change."

"It was clear this morning. I thought we could make it," he said, staring at her like he wanted her to realize he'd tried. And he had. She couldn't fault him. It wasn't his doing that the weather had changed so quickly.

"I know," she said softly, her stomach in knots. "I was disappointed."

"Understand," he said, stepping back, putting distance between them like he feared touching her. "Back to back blizzards in less than a week. I may not have any cattle left."

She stared at him, thinking of what would happen if he lost his cattle while he'd protected her. "They have feed don't they?"

For the last week, she'd been concentrating on getting to her uncle's, not on what Seth had to lose. He could lose his entire herd.

"Yes, but I need to give them hay the next time we get a break," he said, walking toward the bedroom, trunk in hand. "They're depending on me."

She knew he was right and even felt a little selfish for being so concerned about her reputation and not the damage to his life.

There was no sense in worrying about her image any longer because she was a tarnished woman in the eyes of society unless Seth married her. And she didn't need a pity husband. She wanted a man who would love her for who she was and who she hoped to become. Yet thoughts of her and Seth together, the crush of her breasts against his chest, the scent of him assaulting her senses, the feel of his arousal hard against her femininity. Never before had she had such intimate thoughts of a man, not even her fiancé.

A few minutes later, he came out of the bedroom in dry clothes. "I hung up my wet clothes in the bedroom."

"That's fine. It's your room," she said. "I'm just borrowing it until I leave. If I ever leave."

He came up behind her and without turning around, she could smell the essence of Seth. Her body suddenly tingled with an awareness that left her feeling breathless, her skin itching for something she had no experience with. Only that Seth was the man who could give her what she needed.

"I'm heating the leftover chili," she said, trying to keep her attention focused on the dishes in front of her. "I thought I'd warm it up along with the cornbread."

"Sounds good," he said. "What do you want me to do?"

She wanted to tell him, kiss her, but knew that was not a good idea. If he touched her, she would want more and she wasn't even certain of what the more entailed, but when Seth was near, she ached to learn about this primitive connection between a man and a woman.

"You can get out the butter and that jelly you had the other night. That was so sweet and good," she said. This kitchen was such a dangerous area. They could barely move without touching one another, without her nostrils being filled with the scent of virile male and her feminine core responding.

He bumped into her trying to reach the butter and quickly withdrew to the other side of the kitchen. Was he experiencing the same blood heating, stinging sensations to their touch? Was this why he acted as if he didn't want any contact with her?

Sighing, she stopped stirring the pan of chili and turned to gaze at him. "I realize you're tired of me being here, and believe me, I'm ready to go to my uncles and would if I could. That's why I was trying to walk there earlier today."

"It's not that," he said, licking his lips and not really facing her. "Everyone is going to assume that since we spent all this time together that it's only natural that what happens between men and women occurred between us. I'm trying so hard to be an honorable man, but Everleigh, I find you very attractive. I like kissing you. I imagine how beautiful you are all curled up in my bed. I'm fighting this attraction, but it's hard. And when it becomes too much, like last night, I'll go to the barn."

Surprised at his admission, she had to close her mouth as she stared at him in shock. She knew he was a good kisser, but she didn't realize the affect she had on him or that he was attracted to her. And yet like he said, people were going to think what they wanted and there was nothing they could do to stop them, except marry.

"I don't think it's going to matter. I think I'm a ruined woman no matter what," she said. "But I appreciate your honesty and your integrity. You're a good man, Seth."

"You wouldn't think that if you could see the images of us entwined together, naked, in my mind," he said softly.

Her mouth fell open and she stared at him in shock, her heart skipping a beat. How could she respond?

An avalanche of desire swelled within Everleigh, heating her blood and sending smoldering sensations of awareness rippling over her skin. Quickly, she turned back to the stove, trying to focus on their lunch, when all she wanted was to have Seth kiss her, answering the sensual tension that thrummed through her body.

CHAPTER 13

*H*owling accompanied by growling woke Everleigh from a deep sleep. The sound was coming from right outside. Rising from the warm comfort of the bed, she tiptoed across the cold floor to the window and tried to peek outside. She couldn't see anything.

Big Blue barked, the sound loud and deep, threatening.

"Hush," she heard Seth command the dog. But still he gave a deep throated growl.

Something was wrong. A trickle of fear snaked down her spine. Wrapping a blanket around her, she walked to the bedroom door and opened it. The glow of the fireplace an eerie glimmer in the darkened house reflected off the dog who stood at attention beside Seth.

"What's that noise?" she asked.

Seth was pulling his boots on. "A pack of wolves. I think they're trying to find a way into the barn. They must be hungry."

"You're not going out there, are you?" she asked, her heart racing, her chest tightening as she realized the danger.

"I have to protect my livestock," he said, standing to grab his coat off the rack. He gazed at her in the semi-light. "Don't let Big Blue out."

Picking up the rifle sitting by the entrance, he pulled open the door and stepped outside, taking a piece of her heart with him.

Everleigh stood frozen to the spot, shaking as he walked into the snow and cold to face the waiting pack of wolves.

Needing to do something, she put coffee on to heat, knowing he'd be cold when he returned.

At the sound of a shot, she jumped, her chest tightening more as panic clenched her insides.

Big Blue came to her and whined, looking up expectantly, and she sank onto the couch and held the giant dog, giving comfort to the animal and herself.

The growling intensified and another shot rang out in the dark. Then there was silence except for her rapidly beating heart. She wanted to throw open the door, run outside, and make certain he was all right, but worried the dog would take that moment to dash out, and then Seth would have to chase him down in the snow.

For thirty minutes, she waited for him to come back in that door. Fear gnawed at her insides and she wondered if he was safe. At the thought of him injured or hurt or even dying, her chest ached and her heart pounded in her chest.

Seth was a good man she was starting to have feelings for. And now he was out in the snow facing danger, and she hadn't expressed or showed him how she felt. She'd been trying to remain focused on her goal of reaching her uncle and eventually back to New York. Not on the fact that here was a good man she was quickly starting to care about.

And now he was out in the cold and snow, facing danger, alone.

Just when she was about to don warmer clothes and go searching for him, the door opened and Seth walked in.

She ran to him and threw herself in his arms. "I was so scared you'd been hurt."

He held her against his chest, his cold nose pressed against the side of her neck, his lips close to her ear. "They somehow managed to get one of my calves and were fighting over the meat. "I killed two of them before they took off and then I had to bury the bodies in the snow, until I can either burn or drag them far enough away not to attract other animals."

He set the rifle on the floor just as the blanket slipped from her fingers and he pressed into her. "Everleigh..."

Turning her head, his lips found hers, his mouth covering, claiming her with a passion she could no longer deny. A hot, demanding need arose in her clamoring for consummation. Her body thrummed, every nerve tightly wound with an urgency she'd never experienced. She could feel his arousal solid against her center and God, help her, she wanted more than just the feel of him against her pelvis.

One moment, they were standing in the kitchen, and the next, he was swinging her up in his arms, carrying her across the house, through the open doorway of the bedroom. Part of her thrilled at his response, her breathing quickening with anticipation about what was to come.

His lips broke the kiss and he gazed down at her as he dropped her onto the bed. "Tell me now this is not what you want and I'll walk out that door."

Everleigh bit her lip, she could not deny the passion that raced through her blood. She only knew that she ached for the feel of his arms around her, the way his kiss heated her until all she could think about was Seth. The scent of him overpowered her, causing her heart to race. This man had the ability to make her forget all her dreams and plans and want to spend her life with him.

"I want you," she whispered in the darkness, unable to see his eyes, but missing his touch, needing him to quench the fire that raged inside her.

"Everleigh," he groaned, shedding his coat, dropping it onto the floor. "I want you so badly, I'm hurting."

He sank onto the bed beside her, sending shivers rippling along her spine. Was she crazy? She didn't care. She only knew that in this moment, she needed Seth, like she needed her next breath. At his touch, her pulse heated and she reached out to him urgently, wanting to feel his strong arms around her.

He moaned as his mouth descended on hers and he kissed her like a man drowning. His hands gripped her head as he held her mouth open to his and savagely claimed her as his own, his tongue dancing over her lips, caressing her, sending shivers through her as the taste of him flooded her senses, leaving her breathless.

His hands were everywhere, his lips tracing their path as she lay beneath him, while he tantalized and tormented her, tutoring her on desire between a woman and a man.

Sure, she'd been kissed by other men, but never with the passion Seth created. Never like she was his woman, his alone, and he was branding her with his mouth. A moan escaped the back of her throat and he gentled his kiss, his hand skimming over her nightgown to her breasts.

She jumped when he touched her nipple, his hand brushing over the hardened kernel. The heat of his palms scorching her with passion as he caressed her breasts, worshipping her body. If this was so wrong, why did it feel so right?

Needing to feel his flesh, she reached for his shirt, pulling open the buttons, reaching inside to stroke his hard, muscles. Moaning, he yanked his shirt out of his pants as he hauled her against him. "You are so beautiful."

She ran her tongue across the smooth skin of his chest, feeling the muscles ripple from her touch.

"Everleigh," he groaned.

Reaching up, she pulled his mouth down to hers, loving the way his mouth took possession. The feel of his lips caressing her and the slide of his hands down to her breasts had her arching against him, wanting him, needing him. Through her nightgown, she could feel his hardened arousal against the *V* of her legs.

Suddenly he leaped from the bed and shucked his pants, his long johns. Naked, he sank down onto the bed.

"Are you sure?" he asked, while he proceeded to nibble on her neck, his lips hot and moist against the curve of her shoulder, making her even hotter.

She pulled him down for another demanding kiss, showing him what she could not say.

Finally, she released him and he chuckled, his voice low and deep. "Thank goodness."

Lifting the edge of her nightgown, he pulled the silken garment over her head, tossing it aside. Reaching inside her pantaloons, he pushed them down and she kicked them to the floor, knowing there was no turning back. His mouth closed over her nipple, lingering on her breast, he pulled the kernel into the feverish cavern of his mouth, lavishing his tongue around her puckered nipple, suckling until she was moaning and clinging to him, her body in flames. His hand trailed down her chest, across her stomach, his hands plundering her body, touching the very core of her femininity, leaving her gasping and frantic for something she'd never experienced.

With a gasp, she cried out, "Seth."

Sliding his solid body up hers, she felt the heat and hardness of his naked skin gliding across her own. Where he was strong, she was soft, where he was hard, she was silk.

Maybe this was wrong, but it felt so right and her reputation...it was in tatters, what did it matter? Reaching up, she trailed her fingers down his face. Like a blind man, she memorized the hard planes of his features, the scratchiness of his cheeks, the fullness of his lips, the heat in his gaze that burned her to her very core.

This man had taken care of her, he'd fed her, and now...like a punch to the gut, she realized she loved him. During the many days they'd stayed together, during the blizzards, her illness, through it all, he'd been by her side and eventually won her heart.

Pushing her legs apart, he settled between her thighs, the heat of his erection against her center and she lifted her hips, eager to give all of herself to him.

Pulling him closer, she embraced him just as she felt him push into her. With a sharp pain, her maidenhead broke and she gave him her body, her heart, and her soul. Pressing inside her, he committed himself to his passion, possessing her completely.

When she thought she'd never love again, she'd fallen for a rancher in the wilds of Montana. What did she do now?

CHAPTER 14

*S*eth woke before dawn, naked, curled next to Everleigh. Memories from the night before filled his mind, shaking him to his very core. What the hell had he done?

The memory of the wolves, attacking his cattle came rushing back, and the fear that gripped him as he stood in the snow, as not one, but two of the animals charged him. Hungry, they'd seen him as their next meal. And Everleigh had been a welcoming spirit when he'd come in from the cold. Her womanly body had warmed him, comforted him, and been an anchor in the storm.

For over a week, he'd kept his distance from her, protecting his heart and trying to dull the attraction he felt toward this woman, but last night, the attack on his calves opened his eyes. Standing in front of a charging wolf, knowing if his aim was off even a little, he'd never see the woman he cared for again, did things to a man. Made him realize that life was fleeting and could be gone in an instant.

Like a stack of dominoes, she'd easily toppled his willpower, his convictions, and captured his heart and soul.

But now they had done what everyone in town would accuse them of doing and yet he didn't regret spending the night in

Everleigh's arms. But she'd been a virgin. An innocent and he'd deflowered her. If her uncle found out, he'd force him to marry her. Never had he dreamed of a shotgun wedding, but her uncle had every right to demand one.

And he should marry her. They could have created a child last night. His child.

If only Everleigh wanted to marry him. He would take her hand in marriage in a heartbeat. But her dream was that fancy job she was starting in January. She wanted to return to the big city and be a career woman.

He wanted to grow his spread here in Montana, increase his herd and live his life in this wild land. This was his destiny. His place. And no big city could ever give him the life he wanted.

His heart ached at the thought of leaving Montana, but even more knowing that Everleigh would soon be returning to New York. And taking part of him with her.

Catherine had broken his heart when she'd stood him up at the altar, but Everleigh leaving would be even worse. For though he'd thought he loved Catherine, Everleigh was so much more. She was adventurous, fun, and would make some man a terrific help mate. But not him.

And for some reason, that made him sad. Lifting his arm from around her, he knew he had to get away. If the snow had stopped and the sun was shining, he would take her to her uncle's today. Just as soon as the sun rose, he would hitch the sleigh and put as much distance as possible between them. Enough that maybe in time, his heart would heal.

But even now he wanted another night in her arms.

CHAPTER 15

The warmth she had experienced all night long, was gone. Groggily, she rolled over, her eyes flying open as she realized Seth was no longer beside her in bed. Smiling, she remembered the night before. The wolves, the fear, the passion, and the realization that she loved this man came crashing back like an avalanche.

Unable to wait another minute to see Seth, she jumped out of bed, her feet touching the cold floor. Where was he? Why had he left the bed? Why was he no longer beside her?

Slipping on her slippers and nightgown, she opened the door of the bedroom and glanced into the living area. He paced the floor.

Walking up behind him, she laid her hand on his shoulder, loving the feel of the hard muscles beneath her palm. He halted, his muscles stiffening beneath her touch.

"Good morning," she said, smiling, feeling like nothing could destroy her happiness. She loved this man. She loved the way he made her feel. She loved his strong protective nature and the way he took care of her. All of her plans on her big city career didn't seem quite as appealing as Seth.

"Morning," he said, halting in front of the fire. He ran his hand through his hair. "I'm glad you're up. I think we should get an early start this morning. I need to take you to your uncle."

Frowning, she glanced at him, watching him once again pace in front of the fireplace. Was he regretting what had happened between them last night? Had it meant nothing to him?

At the thought of him feeling remorse at their actions, her chest squeezed with a painful tightness that sent chills through her.

"What's the big hurry?" she asked.

His eyes met hers and she could see the uneasiness reflected from deep within him. "I...I thought you would want to be with them as soon as possible?"

"I do," she said. "But after last night..."

Glancing away, he sighed heavily and halted his nervous pacing. "Last night should never have happened. I was wrong to let things get out of hand."

Rage roared through her and tears pricked her eyes and emotions filled her throat. So he did have misgivings about their sweet union. She was in love with him and he suddenly thought of his morals. Heck of a time to have regrets over his actions. Well, fiddlesticks, she couldn't let him see the disappointment and hurt that flooded her soul.

Tilting her head, she tried to think how best to respond. "You are right. Last night was a mistake. Every girl feels bitterness over giving her virginity to the wrong man. Please take me to my uncle's. I'm tired of staying here in this shack you call a home."

She wanted to hurt him like he'd hurt her. She wanted to make him feel small and cheap and everything that rushed like a flood through her veins.

"Yes, ma'am. I'll get the sleigh out and get you to your uncle's."

Striding toward the door, he grabbed his coat and hat and hurried out. She didn't even feel the blast of cold air that filled the room. What had she done? She'd given herself to a man who didn't have emotions. Who cared nothing about her feelings and just wanted her to vacate his home. Once again, he was back to disliking her and she'd given herself to him.

The tears she'd kept at bay flooded down her cheeks and she hastily swiped them away. While she was falling in love with him, he'd suddenly rationalized that they shouldn't have shared passion last night.

Well, that left a hole the size of the Grand Canyon in her chest.

Walking into the bedroom, she changed into a dress, then threw her things in her trunk. Why had she ever decided to come to this God forsaken country? Why hadn't she gone to Texas, instead, and seen her friends? Why was she feeling so lost and helpless, and she hated those emotions. She was a strong woman, and by golly, he was not going to get away with acting this way. He may not love her, he may not want her, but he was not going to brush her off and rush her out the door.

Standing, she went into the front room, pulled on her coat and went to the barn. The sky was cloudy, but snow no longer fell. A blast of cold air hit her and she shriveled inside, trying to hold onto the warmth she'd just left.

Seth was standing between the house and barn, staring at the sky.

"Seth Ketchum," she called as she marched, uncaring, through the snow, her skirt becoming coated with the white powder.

"What are you doing out here? Wait inside until I'm ready to go."

"You are not going to brush me off and treat me like one of your saloon girl trollops."

His mouth curled into a frown and he whirled around to face her. "What are you talking about?"

All the hurt and anger boiled over at the thought he hadn't enjoyed being with her. She loved him and he was not going to toss her aside.

She reached him and pushed her index finger into his chest. "I am not ashamed of what happened between us last night." She pushed her finger into his chest again. "If that makes me a trollop, fine." She poked his chest again. "But don't you ever try to make me feel dirty or ashamed of what happened between us. It was beautiful and wonderful and..."

His mouth slammed down on hers, driving the air from her lungs as he kissed her until she felt faint. Lifting her head, she eagerly gave up to his possession, the feel of his body tightly against her own, his loins pressed into her hard and strong. If the man hadn't enjoyed last night, she certainly couldn't tell from his kiss.

Blood rushed through her, her heart pounded inside her chest, her center warming with all the passion she'd felt last night as she wound her arms around his neck. Whatever had made him skittish was certainly not because the fire that burned between them had cooled.

Finally their lips came apart and she stood in the circle of his arms, her breathing ragged, her chest tight.

"You don't kiss me like you didn't care what we shared," she whispered.

"Last night was great. Too great," he said staring at her, his breath frosting the air. "If I don't take you to your uncle's, we'll soon find ourselves in bed again. You could get pregnant. We'll be forced to marry. All your dreams of your big city job would come to an end. Is that what you want?"

Irritation at the truth of his words left her frustrated. She didn't know what she wanted anymore. Reaching out she shoved him, sending his arms flailing.

"Hey," he yelled as he grabbed onto her and pulled her down with him.

They landed with a thud onto the soft snow with him on bottom and her on top. He rolled her onto her back, his long, lean body stretched on top of her, his face inches from her own.

"Seth," she whispered, feeling every hard inch of him.

"Everleigh, I swear, you're going to be the death of me yet," he whispered against her neck, his mouth lingering.

She tilted her head further back, giving his lips more access to her throat, the warmth of his breath creating shivers of desire pulsing through her.

"You're taking me to my uncle's today," she said, her chest swelling in pain at the thought of being separated from him, but knowing that eventually the time would come for them to part. She had a job to return to and he would stay here in this cold, snowy land.

"The sky isn't clear. I was thinking maybe we would go tomorrow. Today, you could help me feed the cattle that aren't too far from the house. We'll have to keep an eye on the sky to make certain the weather doesn't change, but I could use your help."

She was being given another day with this man she loved. Another day, before they would have to separate and go their own way. One more day to make a lifetime of memories. One more day to decide what she really wanted in life. A life with Seth or to return to her existence in New York.

"Can we get a Christmas tree?"

"What?" he asked, his face scrunched up.

"You know. A small pine tree that we can decorate tonight for Christmas. You don't have any decorations out and well...it's a special time of year."

"I live alone. I didn't see the need for a tree."

"True. But right now, you aren't alone."

With a shrug, he rolled off of her. "All right, but I don't have any store-bought tinsel or ornaments."

"We'll make our own," she said as he gave her a hand up from the snow.

She glanced down at the snow that covered her clothes. "You always seem to find a way to get me wet."

"I like the looks of you wet and snowy, or even better, without clothes," he said and walked away.

For a moment, she stood stunned as a heat rushed to her cheekbones. The man knew just the right words to make her hotter than the Fourth of July in a blizzard.

CHAPTER 16

*H*e was in so much trouble. First, he'd let his passion get away from him and he'd spent the night in Everleigh's arms. Then this morning instead of taking her to her uncle's house, he'd thought just one more day. One more day to spend in her arms before he'd let her go permanently.

So he'd convinced himself they should wait until tomorrow. This afternoon the sun had come out and he knew he could no longer put off what needed doing.

Christmas was in three days and he'd let her persuade him they needed a tree. He was a bachelor. Now, she had him cutting out paper snowflakes to decorate the Christmas tree and remembering Christmases past.

What had he done? During the days she'd been here, he'd gone from a tough man who lived alone to a man who only wanted to please Everleigh. She was turning him into one of those men who doted on their woman. And God, he would love for Everleigh to be his woman in every sense, but knew that was impossible.

Everleigh was a beautiful, strong-willed, determined woman with a career. She wasn't looking for a husband or a family or any of the things he desired. They were polar opposites and yet none of that seemed to matter. All he knew was he wanted her and not long after Christmas, she would be catching the train to New York and her fancy job. Leaving him behind, and if he wasn't careful, with a shattered heart.

What had he been thinking last night? Yet, she was right. It had been a wonderful experience and it was going to be hard to keep his hands to himself. Just once more he'd like to find himself wrapped in her embrace, enjoying the lingering kisses, the heavy throb of his blood, her soft moans that ignited his desire. But he was playing with fire and already suffered from being singed. Tomorrow, he had to make certain she left.

"Seth, look," she cried as she managed to place a makeshift star on top of the tree. "At home, we decorated our tree all together and at the end of the evening, my father put the star on top." She sighed, her eyes filling with tears. "Nothing will ever be the same, will it?"

Memories of Christmas with his family, his mother decorating and his brothers and sisters and his father all gathered together around the table, stabbed his heart with a homesickness he hadn't felt since he left Oregon. Even change for the better could leave you missing what you'd left behind.

"No," he said truthfully. "But you'll always have your memories."

"I didn't know what I had until they were gone," she said.

Leaving Oregon, he'd known he'd miss his family, but hadn't realized how much until he was in Montana. Sure, he could go back, but his life was here and maybe it was time he created his own family and made memories with his wife and future children. Gazing at Everleigh, he wondered about her. There was so much he didn't know about the beautiful woman who intrigued him. If only she wasn't so intent on returning to New York. Could something besides the job be drawing her back to the big city.

"Why weren't you at the apartment the night of the accident?"

he asked. His sister Grace would have been home at the time of the explosion. Why wasn't Everleigh?

She laughed a sardonic sound and shook her head. "Because I was out with my fiancé. The man I was supposed to marry, only he chose that night to end our relationship. Seemed he didn't think I was ready for marriage," she snorted. "But Kelsey Jones was ready and he married her not six weeks after we ended our engagement."

Was this man the reason she was returning to New York? But he was married.

"Did you love him," he asked, his feelings mixed regardless of how she responded. He didn't want her to love another man.

"At the time, I thought so. But now, I'm not so certain," she answered honestly as she hung another snowflake on the tree.

"Don't you think you were better off that he ended the engagement before you married him?"

"Yes, but I was in shock coming home to the block surrounded by firemen and police, no home and no place to go, and worst of all, no family. I lost everything that night," she said, her voice cracking. "It would have been nice to have someone to lean on during that difficult time. I had no one. Not even my aunt and uncle."

"I'm sorry. I didn't know you'd lost so much in one night," he said, watching the expression on her face, wanting to go to her, pull her into his arms and tell her it was all right. "What did you do?"

Biting her lip, she turned back to the tree and hung the snowflake he'd created on a branch. Then she faced him. "I went to a friend's house who took me in. For the next two weeks, I was busy with funeral arrangements, the wills, searching through the rubble for anything left."

"What did you find?" he asked, thinking it was a morbid question, but curious if she found anything that would give her comfort.

"I found my mother's jewelry box that held her diamonds and my father had given me his pocket watch to make certain I came home on time. That's all I have left," she said, her eyes shadowed with pain, her face white. In the glow of the fireplace, he could see the grief reflected in her beautiful green eyes and his heart ached for her.

"I wish I'd been there to hold you, comfort you," he said quietly, knowing there was no way he was staying out of her bed tonight. He needed to wrap his arms around her. He wanted these last few hours with Everleigh.

She looked up at him, smiling. "I do, too." Sighing, she grabbed a piece of paper and tried to appear chipper. "Let's make a Christmas wish."

Frowning, he wasn't certain what she wanted, but at this moment, he would do anything to make her happy. "What do you mean?"

"Let's write our wishes on a piece of paper and hang them on the tree. Then on Christmas morning, we'll look at them."

"I doubt you'll be here on Christmas morning, but we can do that if you want."

"You can't peek, but you can bring them to my aunt and uncle's house."

Quickly, she cut the paper in half, folded it, and punched a small hole with a knitting needle. She attached a piece of thread through to tie it to the tree and handed the paper to him. Knowing what he really wanted to write on that paper, but uncertain she was ready to hear the words, he quickly wrote his carefully worded feelings on the ornament.

When she finished, she stood and he followed her lead. Together, they hung their wishes on the tree she had beautifully decorated. She'd made his tiny house feel like a home and he hadn't had that experience since leaving Oregon.

Knowing he was in so much trouble, but unable to stop himself he pulled her into his arms, her scent wrapping around him like an aphrodisiac creating a burning sensation that heated his blood. Everleigh drew out the best in him, made him a better man, turned his house into a home.

The past days had been more fun, all because she made him laugh. She smiled and teased and made him happy. Returning to his old way of living would be difficult and yet wasn't that what he wanted? To be single and alone and living off the land? Why did the idea of following her to New York sound better and better, and yet he knew he could never be happy there. This was his home. But he didn't want to let Everleigh go.

"Let's go to bed, Everleigh," he whispered as he nuzzled her neck, already drunk on the taste of her skin, thinking of the passionate night ahead and dreading the days beyond.

CHAPTER 17

*T*he next morning she awoke to bright sunlight streaming through the window and didn't know if she should feel happy or sad. Her gut clenched and she knew in her heart he would take her to her uncle's today. Just as soon as he checked on his herd, Seth would insist it was time for her to leave, before her reputation was completely unsalvageable. And yet right now, she didn't care.

Lying there, thinking about the night before, her heart burst. They'd made love, not once but twice and each time, she fell deeper and deeper in love with him. How could she go off and leave? After what they'd shared, she couldn't imagine never seeing him again and yet, her lifelong dream of being a journalist was in New York.

With a twinge, her conscience reminded her it was a typing position, but she hoped eventually the paper would see her abilities as a writer and let her become a journalist. But what were the odds of them taking someone from their typists and seeing them anywhere but behind that new-fangled machine newspapers now used.

Giving up her dream of being a journalist would be heart wrenching. And yet, losing Seth would be worse.

Without knowing the answer and realizing he hadn't even asked her to marry him, it would be difficult to toss her dreams aside. He may not share the feelings that were growing within her, causing her so much confusion. Jumping out of bed, she went in search of the man she loved.

Opening up the door to the main section of the house, she saw a note sitting on the table.

Everleigh,

I went to feed the cattle. When I return, we need to talk.

Seth

A tremor of apprehension scurried down her spine. The note had an ominous tone. Hurriedly, she dressed, preparing herself for the discussion she was certain would either bring them closer or tear them apart. She made a pot of coffee, knowing that while the sun was shining brightly, the temperature was still cold. Seth would appreciate a hot cup of coffee to chase away the chill and it was something she could do for him.

The sleigh drove into the yard, just as the coffee finished brewing. Fixing him a cup, she waited, but he didn't appear.

Finally, she bundled up and hurried outside. The chill bit her to the bone as she walked the thirty feet to the building she could now see clearly in the sunshine.

Walking inside, it was obvious he'd been busy this morning. The animals all had fresh hay, oats, and water. Glancing around the barn the building appeared empty.

"Seth?"

"Up here," he said, and she glanced up to see him in the hayloft.

"Did you feed your cows?"

"Yes," he said, his voice sounding strained.

Funny how she knew something troubled him. With a determined stride, she hurried to the ladder that led to the loft and hastily climbed before he could protest.

When she reached the top, she crawled onto the hayloft.

"What are you doing?" he said as he spied her from where he was pitching hay down below.

"I came to see you," she said, and stared at the man she'd shared the most intimate act on earth with. Something worried him and she wanted to ease the way his brow was furrowed, his blue eyes darkening at the sight of her. There was a quiet gentleness about him that intrigued her. Yet she knew from experience, he was a commanding man with a stubborn streak for righteousness. "You were gone when I woke."

He swallowed and pitched a forkful of hay out the opening of the barn. "I had to check on the cattle."

"Were they all right?"

"They were hungry and happy to see me," he said.

He dropped the pitchfork and walked toward her, a serious expression on his face.

She knew immediately in her gut what he was going to say and she wasn't ready to hear the words. She didn't want to listen to reason and she didn't want to face the realities of what they'd done unless he said the words she longed to hear. These days together had been idyllic and even now she didn't want them to end.

Reaching behind her, she grabbed a handful of hay. When he neared her, she tossed the straw at him.

"What was that for?" he sputtered.

"Because," she said, not willing to say the words, wanting to put off this discussion for as long as possible. "Because I can. Because I saw that serious look in your eyes, and I don't want to face what you're going to say."

"We need to talk."

"Not yet," she said.

Shaking his head, he reached down and she knew he was

going to retaliate, so she ran. Sprinting across the loft, she scurried to the far corner, where there were several bales of the loose straw. Hiding behind the bundled straw, she drew back her arm and threw several handfuls at him. Walking toward her with a purpose, the strands of the dried grass, bounced off his coat, pants, and fell to the ground at his feet.

That little sputtering of hay didn't slow him as he continued toward her, his stride confidant and secure. With nowhere to run, she tried to dart to the side, but he reached out and wrapped his fingers around her arm. With a toss, she landed onto a bed of loose hay. Dropping down beside her, he began to cover her with the straw.

"What are you doing?" she laughed.

"I'm burying you," he said, reaching out and tickling her, sending the dried grass everywhere. "This way you won't ever leave this barn."

She laughed out loud, throwing her head back, until he landed on top of her, swishing the air from her lungs. Every inch of his rock-hard male body pressed against her as heat poured through her veins, leaving her gasping. Staring into the warmth of his blue eyes, losing herself in his gaze, she wondered how she could live without him.

"Oh, Mr. Ketchum, I see straw excites you," she said, reaching up and pulling his face closer to her, her breathing ragged as her nipples hardened, her womanly body softening, responding to his masculinity.

"No, you excite me. I can't keep my hands off you, even in the hayloft," he said, nuzzling her neck, licking her earlobe, sending delightful shivers coursing through her.

She let out a long sigh as his mouth covered hers. Once again, her body responded to his kiss in a way that snatched her breath away, her heart racing as his lips lit a fire inside her that drove the cold from the barn. She lifted her arms and wrapped them around Seth's neck, aching with the knowledge that soon she'd be gone. Soon she'd never see him again and her chest tightened and burned with unshed tears.

Releasing her mouth, his hands reached inside her coat and pulled her dress down far enough to give him access to her breasts. Swirling his tongue around her hardened nipple, he pulled the pebble into his mouth, sending a rush of desire scorching through her.

"Oh, Seth," she moaned. Reaching for his belt, she quickly unbuckled the leather, unbuttoned his pants and reached inside, wanting, needing to touch him once more. Just once more to be joined together.

"Everleigh," he moaned. "We can't do this again."

"I want you," she said against his throat, knowing she craved him one last time.

Like her worst nightmare ever, she heard a man's voice calling out. "Seth. Seth you up there?"

Seth froze on top of her, her hands inside his pants, his mouth on her breasts. He cursed. "We're in trouble."

"Who is it?" she asked, wondering if it was her uncle.

Shaking his head, he stood and quickly buttoned his pants. "I'm here, preacher. I'll be right down."

"The preacher?" she asked, her heart skipping a beat and then racing like wild to catch up, leaving her nauseous and faint.

"None other," he said, and slowly crawled over the side of the hayloft.

CHAPTER 18

$\mathcal{S}$eth climbed down the ladder and realized he couldn't go off and leave Everleigh up there alone. The woman could trip and fall on her skirt, coming down the ladder.

"Just a minute, preacher," he said and then went halfway back up the ladder. "Everleigh, come down."

She'd already pulled her dress back into place and now she shook the hay off her skirt and blouse and tried to get it out of her hair. But it was everywhere. There was no hiding what they'd been doing.

"Let me help you down. I don't want you to fall," he said, watching her hesitancy. Shaking her head, she swung a leg over the ladder and he quickly moved out of the way.

Standing below, but close enough to catch her if she fell, he watched her crawl down the ladder. When she was safely on the ground, they both faced the preacher who looked like he would faint.

"Good morning," she said.

The man's eyes were wide, his mouth hanging open as he stared at the two of them. Finally, he took a deep breath. "You didn't make it to your uncle's?"

Seth glanced at Everleigh and then the preacher. "No, sir, it was snowing so hard, we barely made it here."

"And you've been here the entire time?"

"Yes, sir," Everleigh said, her eyes staring at him, her body rigid. "We had no choice. It was either continue on and risk dying or stay at Seth's. We chose to live."

For a woman who had first doubted his decision to stop at his home instead of continuing on, she was doing a fine job of defending him. Even at the cost to her reputation, could that mean she would be open to his proposal of marriage?

The man's lips pursed into a taut line. "Seth, can I speak to you outside."

"Whatever you're going to say to him, you can say it here in front of me," Everleigh replied.

While Seth admired her spunk, now was not the time and he was certain he knew what the preacher was going to say to him. She would completely lose her composure at the mere mention of marriage. He wasn't going to embarrass her or himself in front of the man from his church.

Reaching over he patted her on the arm. "Give us just a moment, Everleigh, then we can all talk."

"The answer is no," she said belligerently. "No, I'm not being forced to get married and no, not..."

Her voice trailed off and the preacher's eyes widened. Sometimes women would be better off if they kept their mouth shut and let him handle the situation. Yes, she was responding exactly like he'd known she'd react. She didn't want to marry a rancher. She wanted a big city career and probably a banker as well. He was fooling himself if he thought they had a chance at marriage.

Leading the preacher out of the barn, Seth left Everleigh in the building smoldering with resentment. Sighing, he said, "Follow me, Bart. Did you go up to the house? I'd been out feeding the cattle and then I had plans on taking Everleigh to her uncle's this afternoon. But my cattle were starving and I had to take care of them."

It was true. Just as soon as he'd finished filling up the hay barrel he'd been intent on taking Everleigh to her uncle's today. But sometimes God had a mean streak and they'd been caught. Almost *flagrant delicto*. If Bart had come five minutes later, his ears would have probably burned from the noises he would have heard coming from the hayloft.

The preacher was quiet as they made their way to his sleigh, the cold breeze stinging their exposed skin. Finally, he halted by his vehicle and cleared his throat. "Seth, you're a good man. But you've compromised this young woman and you know as a Christian and a man of faith what you need to do."

The man was saying the very words his mother would have said to him. He'd thought about it all morning long while he fed the cattle, but Everleigh didn't want him. She had no desire to live here in Montana and he was not going to follow her back to the big city.

"I know what I should do, but she doesn't want me permanently."

"She could be with child. Your child. She will be considered a ruined and defiled woman. An outcast from church and society. You need to do what's right," he said softly, giving Seth a fatherly glance. "Obviously, she felt something for you. Let me know when. I can marry you two anytime."

Seth watched as he climbed up in his sleigh. "There's been an outbreak of measles in town. It's the reason I stopped to check on you before I drove out to James and Myrtle's house. It's my duty to tell her uncle what I saw today. I'll tell him he can expect the two of you later this afternoon."

"Yes, sir," Seth said really not liking this man at the moment. Sure, he'd been wrong, but it was a delicious wrong. One that was probably going to break his heart and make him an outcast in town. Now he had to go back into the barn and tell Everleigh her uncle would know the truth when they arrived.

"The town is just starting to recover from the epidemic. We're having a town celebration for Christmas. I hope to see you two there as man and wife. Let's avoid a Mistletoe scandal."

CHAPTER 19

*S*eth marched back into the barn. He'd been such a fool. First with Catherine and now Everleigh. Catherine, he'd blindly believed they were in love and she wanted to marry him. Everleigh, because the woman made him forget his principles.

She made him forget everything but the perfect way she fit against his body as he held her in his arms, the smell of roses and lavender that filled the air around her and the way she had him discussing everything from politics to women's clothes. In the last ten days, he'd smiled and laughed more than he had since being stood up at the altar.

And now it had come crashing to an end.

Slamming the barn door, the animals all jerked their heads up from their feed to gaze in bewilderment, while Everleigh hurried over to him.

"What did he say?"

"What any preacher would say. That I should marry you."

She didn't respond.

Licking his lips, he stared at her. "I was going to talk to you later this morning, when I came in from the barn. I think we should get married."

"Why?" she asked. "And are you willing to move to New York?"

"No. I have a home. A ranch, everything right here. We could live here."

"And I have a job," she said, biting her lip. "I've never lived anywhere besides New York."

"You have family here," he said. "There's no one waiting for you in New York."

He watched her wringing her hands. What was he doing? Trying to persuade a woman who didn't love him to marry him was not the marriage his parents experienced.

"You could be with child, even now," he said softly. But he didn't want her to marry for that reason.

Call him old fashioned, but he wanted her to marry him because she'd fallen in love. He'd watched his parents' marriage. Love had poured from the two of them. Sure, they fought, but they also kissed, laughed, and made up. That was what he wanted. Not a woman forced to marry him, but because she wanted to spend the rest of her days at his side.

She held up her hand. "I refuse to consider that possibility. I can't deal with the thought of being pregnant and alone."

He couldn't either. He didn't want to take a chance. He wanted Everleigh to marry him.

"You wouldn't be alone. It would be my child just as much as yours. And it would have my name."

She walked out of the barn and he followed. "If you're pregnant, we're getting married."

She whirled around to face him. "Nobody is telling me what to do. I'll be back in New York, so you'll never know."

Damn, she could be difficult. But he was not going to give up. "I'll find out."

"If we marry, I will have agreed to your proposal. Which I haven't heard yet."

What was wrong with her. Did she think he was going to get down on bended knee with the preacher watching? Had she considered that he would want to speak to her uncle before he asked for her hand? Did she ever consider that he would want to try to make his proposal special? Or did she just want to hop on that train back to New York and forget him.

"Well, pardon me, but I'm not exactly in the mood to get down and go through the motions of asking you to be my wife."

As soon as the words left his mouth, he knew that was the wrong thing to say. Her jaw dropped open and she tensed. Then turned and started walking to the house again.

"Good, because I would say no," she shouted.

He hurried after her, knowing he had to calm her. "Everleigh, we're both upset. Let's take a deep breath, settle down and discuss this like two people who are making a business decision. We can lay out everything we both expect in a marriage on the table and come to an agreement."

She turned and stared at him, shaking her head. "You just don't get it, do you? I'm not marrying anyone who is stupid enough to think I'm going into this like a business arrangement. That's not what I want in life and I don't care if I am pregnant. At least I'll be raising _MY_ baby without a father who has no emotion in a civilization where the blizzards don't last forever," she said, her voice rising in volume.

They were standing between the house and the barn yelling at each other. But worse, this was not how he'd intended the conversation to go. He'd imagined them sitting down at the table discussing the problem like the adults he'd assumed they were, but instead he could see the anger rising inside her and wondered why.

Why was she so enraged? Fifteen minutes ago, they'd been

tearing at each other's clothes, now they were screaming at one another. What had happened to change things?

Hands on hips, she glared at him. "My trunk is ready to load and as soon as I freshen up a bit, I'll be ready to leave."

CHAPTER 20

The ride to her uncle's was the longest and the shortest hour of her life. Long because they said very little to each other, their earlier words hanging like a weight around her heart. Did the man have no emotion? Did he feel nothing for her and yet they'd spent what she thought were magical days and nights together.

Short because she dreaded facing her uncle and his disapproval. It had been years since she'd seen him and her aunt Myrtle. Years, and now during her toughest holiday season in her life, she'd ruined her reputation and fallen in love.

They turned down the drive and nerves tightened her stomach into a ball. She'd never been to her aunt and uncle's home. She'd only visited with them when they came to New York, which hadn't been since she was a little girl. But still this was her father's brother, her uncle, her only family. She wondered how he would react.

"I want to talk to your uncle alone," Seth said.

For the last hour, he hadn't said a word, and now opening his mouth, he'd just made her angrier. "No."

Her future was not being decided behind closed doors or

without her. They couldn't make her marry. She refused to wed anyone unless they loved her.

"We'll see," he said, snapping the reins to urge the horses faster.

Soon, they were pulling up in front of the house and she'd never missed her mother more. If the explosion had never happened, she'd still be in New York and this would all be nothing more than a bad dream.

Her aunt and uncle stepped onto the porch, their faces grim.

When the sleigh came to a halt, she didn't wait for Seth to help her, but climbed down on her own. Walking carefully through the snow to the porch, she hurried up the steps, ignoring Seth. "Aunt Myrtle, Uncle James, so glad to see you. Where are the children?"

Her aunt came and hugged her, but her uncle stood glaring at Seth.

"It's good to see you. The children are inside. We told them to wait inside so we could have a chance to talk."

"How are you feeling, Uncle James?"

"I'm fine," he said glaring at Seth. This couldn't be good.

Maybe they didn't want her around their kids. Maybe they were afraid her evilness would spill onto their little darlings that she hadn't even met. Well, if that was the case, she'd find a way back into town and leave this wretched place. Or maybe they just wanted a chance to talk openly without the children hearing what was going on.

Taking a deep breath, she tried to calm her rapidly beating heart and think logically and sensibly instead of reacting on emotion. Standing on the porch, they watched Seth unload her trunk from the sleigh and carry it up to the porch.

"Thank you," she said politely and turned away dismissing him.

"James. Myrtle," he said. He stood with his hat in his hands in front of her uncle. "I'd like to speak privately with you."

The man refused to listen to her and just didn't give up. To salvage his manly pride and his righteousness, he was going to offer to marry her. She didn't need his pity offer.

"Boy, I've been thinking of ways I could hurt you. I'm tempted to pull out my shotgun and make you do the honorable thing of marrying my niece."

"No," Everleigh said as all eyes turned to her. "I'm not marrying a man who doesn't want me."

Glancing back to Seth, they ignored her.

"Sir, I understand. But I need to speak with you in private."

Everleigh stepped out of her aunt's embrace, pushing away. "No. You're not talking to him without me being there. Uncle James, do not do this."

Her uncle frowned at her. "Everleigh, this is between men. Go in the house with your aunt."

Her aunt took her by the arm and led her away. "Come on, Everleigh, it's best to let the men hash this out."

The only way she could stay was to make a scene as her aunt had a grip on her arm like a sheriff hauling in a criminal.

"I'm not marrying him," she said vehemently. "No one is going to force me to do anything."

"I know you're upset," her aunt said calmly. "Come in the kitchen and let's make a cup of soothing tea. You can tell me what happened. All we know is that the preacher found the two of you together this morning in a compromising situation."

Though still as nice as she remembered, her aunt was one of those typical women who believed that men were the chosen ones and a woman was to be subservient to her husband. Not Everleigh. But since she was in a rather precarious position, she followed her aunt, sending Seth one last blistering glance before she went inside.

"It wasn't Seth's fault," Everleigh said. "It was the weather. We've been stuck in that little house of his since I arrived."

Her aunt's eyes grew large. "We thought you were in town."

"No, he picked me up and we started to your house but before we reached his home, the snow was falling so thick, you couldn't see. I've been there since my train arrived."

Aunt Myrtle, laid her hand on her arm and pushed her gently into a kitchen chair. "Did the two of you have sexual relations?"

She'd planned on lying. She'd even thought she could get away without telling anyone, but that darn preacher man had messed up her carefully laid out plans. There was no denying what had happened between her and Seth.

"Yes, we did."

"Then you have to marry him," her aunt said softly.

A tear welled up in her eye and then another, and another. "But he doesn't love me. He thinks we should make a business arrangement." She shuddered. "I'm not marrying anyone I don't love."

Tears rolled unheeded down her cheeks.

"Do you love him?"

Biting her lip, she tried not to sob. "Yes."

CHAPTER 21

*A*fter Seth left, her uncle came into the kitchen, a grim expression on his face.

"It's all set. You'll be married on Christmas Eve."

"Absolutely not," she said rising. "No one is making me marry that man."

This was not how she wanted to marry. A girl had dreams of a man proposing, telling her he loved her, and offering a ring. She'd already experienced that once and while the marriage hadn't occurred, she still had hope that eventually the right man would offer for her hand. This was not the way a lasting marriage of love and commitment began and she refused to settle for anything less.

Her aunt shook her head. "Everleigh, why not? You just told me you love him."

Tears once again filled her eyes and she refused to cry. "Because...because he doesn't love me. I'm not marrying someone who doesn't love me. I want a marriage like my parents had, not a cold, loveless union all because everyone's afraid I'm expecting. How could that be a good place to raise a child. Children need two parents who love one another. What good would it do me?"

"You've got to marry him," her uncle said, his voice filled with conviction. "Your reputation is at stake. Everyone in town will learn that you stayed at his home for ten days. It doesn't matter that you had no choice. They will assume, and it will be true that something happened between the two of you. You've got to marry."

"No," she said, determination for what she wanted making her sound short and angry. "I'll just get on the next train back to New York and never come back to Mistletoe."

Sighing, her uncle stared at her. "Bad news spreads faster than a wildfire. Eventually, this will get back to New York. And if you're pregnant, it won't matter as it will be obvious. Just marry him."

Wouldn't she feel different if she were pregnant? Wouldn't she know? Yes, it was way too early to know for certain, but still the only thing different was her heart breaking.

All Seth had to do was tell her that he loved her and she would have married him, but instead he'd wanted to make a business arrangement. Was she a profit or loss? Or was she just the hired help. How could she reside in the same house, seeing him each day, knowing that she loved him. She wanted to be his equal, his partner, his helpmate, his lover, and so far there had been no declarations, no acknowledgements, nothing but his pity offer.

"I have a job, a place to live, and a life in New York. I'm not willing to give that up for a man who can't express his emotions," she said softly.

Shaking his head, her uncle said quietly, "What would your father do if he'd been alive and this happened?"

She started to cry, missing her mother and the way she always managed to find a solution when a problem came up. "He'd make me marry."

"I can't let you go back to New York, not knowing if you're pregnant and unmarried, with a scandal attached to your name.

Your father would haunt me for the rest of my life because I didn't do what was right for his daughter. You have to marry Seth. He's agreed to let you return to New York after the wedding."

Anger like the blowing winds of the blizzard blew through her, leaving her madder than a hell cat. Taking a deep, calming breath, she sighed. So he'd marry her and let her go back to New York - he didn't love or want her.

Did no one understand that what she needed wasn't complicated or even asking too much? All she longed for was some heartfelt emotion from Seth that showed her he loved her and desired her as his wife, because of his love - not the scandal.

"Did he mention the word love?" she said, her voice trembling with hurt.

"No. But Seth is not the type of man who wears his emotions on his sleeve and he's not one for talking to other men about his feelings. But he wouldn't marry you if he didn't care about you and your reputation."

"He is only doing this because his conscious is telling him it's the right thing. And the chance that there could be a child. Not that he cares about me. I'm a duty, an obligation."

Her aunt patted her on the arm. "You don't know that. But if you marry him, then you will repair the damage done to your reputation and protect the babe you could be carrying. I got pregnant on my wedding night with your uncle."

Everleigh stared at her aunt and licked her lips. She really hadn't given the thought of being with child any real consideration. She just didn't believe it could happen to her and she didn't feel any different, except for the pain around her heart. Would it be fair to have a child labeled as a bastard all because she'd been too stubborn to marry its father?

While she still didn't believe she was pregnant, it would be a little late once she reached New York to reconsider. And she did love Seth. But she would be forever tied to a man who lived in

Montana, if she married him and then returned to New York. But if she married him, she could never marry and if she wasn't pregnant, then she would be alone the rest of her life.

"I'll think about it. I'm not saying yes or no. But I'll consider marrying him just to protect the child I could be carrying."

Frowning, her uncle hugged her. "He'll be here at eleven tomorrow to discuss the details."

CHAPTER 22

*T*hat night, Seth thought he would go crazy, walking around in his small empty house that now felt gigantic without Everleigh. The rooms that once had been his haven of peace and solace were now empty chambers that lacked the warmth and vitality they'd once held. And his bed was such a lonely place, he'd finally moved back to the couch.

Everything had changed and he no longer felt at home in his own place. Sometimes he thought he could smell Everleigh, her perfume seemed to linger in the air where she had walked from room to room. He wanted to chase after that scent and hold onto her fragrance before it dissipated.

Glancing up from the fire where he'd been sitting and staring aimlessly, he saw the tree. That damn Christmas tree she'd insisted on bringing into the house. The paper snowflakes, the crooked star, and the paper wishes hanging from the limbs a reminder of a great night. She'd insisted they each write down a wish they would open on Christmas morning.

Well, he wasn't waiting. He wanted to read hers now. He knew what he'd written on his. And if he had his way, she would read it on Christmas morning.

He strode to the tree and yanked her wish from the limb. As he opened the paper, a chill went through him. Shocked, he stared at the message, his heart seizing in his chest.

My Christmas Wish

May the next few weeks clear the confusion from my head and heart and my parents' spirits guide me in the direction my life should take. And may the spirit of Christmas with its fulfillment of new beginnings and hope fill Seth. Everleigh.

Stunned, he stared at the note. Was she just as confused as he was? Sure, he'd had his heart broken once before, but it wasn't because of something he'd done. He'd had no control over Catherine making the decision to run away with a man she'd just met. And maybe, as his father liked to say, he'd gotten the luck of the draw, because if he'd married Catherine, he'd never have met Everleigh.

Still, was he willing to take a chance on Everleigh? Would she keep him waiting at the church?

A shiver ran down his spine at the memory of standing in front of the church, waiting, while his heart slowly shriveled in front of everyone. The weeks following, the looks from people in town, the whispers. He'd known Catherine for nearly eighteen years and Everleigh for fewer than two weeks. Was he crazy? If he agreed to marry her, could he trust her not to leave him facing a congregation of sad faces?

Even in the short days they'd been together, he'd fallen in love with Everleigh. He loved the way she seemed to fill a room and make it sunny and bright, even on a dark snowy day. The way she drew him out of his shell and how easy she made it for him to talk to her. The way she never shut up, which could be irritating and wonderful at the same time.

Stuck here in this cabin for ten days, he'd seen the best of her and the worst of her, and well, she made him a better man. He'd laughed, he'd loved and experienced more happiness in those ten days than many people experienced in a lifetime. He'd never felt more alive than while she was challenging him and not letting him retreat into himself.

Sure, he wanted what was best for her, but he also knew that maybe he was good for her as well. Maybe she needed him like he needed her.

With sudden clarity, he realized he couldn't let her go without trying one more time. They'd both said a lot of things in anger, but now that they'd had time to settle down, maybe they could talk sensibly. But would she be willing to give up her big city career and live a quiet life with him in the backwoods of Montana. Raise some kids and build a life together. He hoped so.

If she didn't have that big city job and the longing for a career, he knew this wouldn't be a question. A job at a newspaper...the memory of Tom Stuart with that ridiculous contraption around his neck came to mind. Tom owned the local paper. Tom was a small operation, but still who wrote the articles in his paper? What if he needed a journalist? A woman's perspective on life in Montana.

Tomorrow morning, he'd go to town and see if the local newspaper was looking to hire a female journalist. If he could keep Everleigh in Montana and fulfill her dreams of being a journalist, while being his wife, nothing would make him happier. For a chance with her, he'd stand in front of a church once again, waiting, hoping, praying she would show up.

He'd been willing to marry her and let her return to New York, but maybe, just maybe they had a chance of being married and being happy together right here in Mistletoe.

He walked back to the tree and pulled off his Christmas wish. Had he known even then that he loved Everleigh? Glancing down, he read what he wrote.

Oh, yes, he'd known she'd wrangled his heart, but been unable to face the fact that he loved her and she would leave him.

CHAPTER 23

*E*verleigh didn't know whether to laugh or cry. Seth had told her uncle, he'd be there at eleven, it was now after two and he'd yet to show up. So much for him wanting to marry her. Her aunt glanced at her nervously like she was going to go into a fit of the vapors. But Everleigh didn't do vapors.

When the pain of life was at its worst, she picked up her needlepoint, losing herself in the stitches. And so far today, she'd almost finished a seat cushion as she sat on the couch waiting, listening to the clock tick-tock like a hammer hitting a nail.

She stood, unable to wait any longer. "I'm going to go lie down. It's obvious he's not coming."

"Maybe something happened," her aunt said. "Maybe there's been an accident."

"And maybe he doesn't want to marry me," she said, rising from the rocking chair.

Her uncle had limped outside and was busy swinging his chop ax, splitting logs, doing more resting than chopping. She almost envied him the task, thinking how each blow to the log would be exerting frustration and anger. Tomorrow, she promised herself she was going to wake up and be prepared to celebrate the Christmas spirit and put all this behind her.

Her parents would want her to celebrate this holy time. Life moved on whether they were at her side or not, and life would continue without Seth's love.

"Don't give up on him, just yet," her aunt replied. "Men can be stubborn."

Everleigh flipped her hand at her aunt in a gesture of *it's over*. She was done with the drama and tension, and frankly, she just wanted her peaceful life back. But now she'd have a scandal tied to her name.

"I'll be taking a nap."

Walking into the bedroom, she heard the sound of bells jingling coming down the lane. She peered out the window and saw Seth driving the sleigh trimmed with garland and silver bells. He was certainly all decked out for the holidays. Yet, she just didn't feel the spirit and she'd made up her mind. She wasn't marrying him, unless he told her he loved her.

Regardless that she loved him, she was holding out for a man who loved and wanted her.

Sitting on the bed, she heard her aunt and uncle invite him into their home. Maybe she should stay inside her room and refuse to see him because she feared he wasn't going to say the words that would make her commit to him. And without those three little words, there was no reason for them to continue talking.

Her aunt knocked on the door. "Everleigh, Seth's here."

"Tell him to go away."

Her aunt opened the door and peered in. "You have to speak with him."

"No, I don't and I won't."

If she didn't, how would she ever know if he cared? She would wonder the rest of her life if she'd walked away from love.

With a sigh, she rose from the bed. "All right, he's got five minutes."

She strolled into the parlor of her aunt and uncle's small house, doing her best to remain aloof and appear calm. "Seth."

"Everleigh, you're looking beautiful."

"Thank you," she said, wondering if they would continue to talk like two strangers. "I thought you were going to be here at eleven?"

"That was my intentions, but I had to go to town."

She nodded, trying her best not to act like she cared, when inside her heart was swelling with love and longing for this man. And all she had to do was say yes and he would be hers for eternity without the one emotion she needed to hear him express.

"Everything is arranged. We're to be wed tomorrow night at seven o'clock in the church. There's going to be a huge party to celebrate the new doctor saving so many lives from the measles epidemic. So our wedding will be the highlight of the celebration."

Did he just say what she thought? He'd assumed that she would agree to be his wife and marry him without even asking her? What was wrong with him?

She stared at him incredulously. "What? You arranged for our wedding before I agreed to marry you?"

He licked his lips and shuffled nervously, but his gaze never left hers. "I know you may or may not say yes. I could be left standing at the altar once again, but I wanted to show you that I'm serious. I want to marry you. Your uncle mentioned you might marry me and return to New York."

He sighed. "I know you have a big impressive job waiting for you back in New York, but I thought maybe I could get you the same type of job here. No, it wouldn't be for a worldwide newspaper, but it would still be doing what you love. I spoke to Tom and he's agreed to hire you as a journalist for the newspaper. All you have to do is write one article a week for the Mistletoe Gazette. As my wife, you're not expected to work, but if you want to, you can."

Her mouth fell open and her insides clenched at the realization of what he'd done. He'd gotten her a job, and not as a typist, but an actual journalist writing articles. Her dream position that she didn't even have in New York. She would be writing for a newspaper.

"That's why I was late. It came to me last night that maybe you could do what you loved right here in Mistletoe."

"Seth," she whispered, her heart clenching. He'd thought about her enough to get her a job, but he still hadn't said those three little words she needed to hear.

"I know our courtship wasn't the normal kind. And we've only known each other for days. But I don't want you to leave. I want you to stay and marry me."

She kept gazing at him, waiting, and wondering if he was going to express his emotions, or if he was unable to say the words she needed to hear to convince her to marry him.

He clenched his fist. "I'm not very good at this. But I wanted to tell you, I will be at the church tomorrow at seven, waiting. You think about it and meet me there if you want to get married."

Reaching into his pocket, he pulled out his Christmas Wish. "I know it's not Christmas yet, but I brought our Christmas wishes and thought they should be on your aunt and uncle's tree."

Why had he brought their Christmas wishes? She remembered what she'd written on hers, knowing even then that she loved him, undecided about how she wanted this time to end. Did she want to return to New York and her job or did she want to stay and be Seth's wife. She'd expressed her confusion on her Christmas wish and asked for clarity.

Walking to the tree, he hung the two wishes and then turned to face them.

"I have to go. I have animals to feed before it gets dark." He glanced at Everleigh. "I'll be waiting at the church tomorrow night."

CHAPTER 24

*E*verleigh stared at the closed door Seth had just walked through. The man was the most aggravating, irritating, unemotional man she'd ever met and she loved him with all her heart. Trying to keep her here, he'd found her a job. Not a typist position, but a genuine actual journalist writing for the newspaper. And it made her love him even more.

But he still hadn't said that magical phrase.

"That boy is confounded," her aunt said. "I think he loves you, but just hasn't said the words."

"He doesn't realize that you women need to hear them words before you can commit to a man." His uncle shook his head. "And I'm not going to be the one to enlighten him. This one he's got to figure out for himself."

Everleigh stood listening to her aunt and uncle and wondered what should she do. He didn't say he loved her, yet his actions spoke like a man in love. He'd driven into town and gotten her dream job. He'd made the arrangements and even put himself waiting at the church for her to appear, after he'd already been left humiliated waiting at the altar. It was like he was doing everything, but not saying the actual words and taking a huge risk to suffer once again the same embarrassment.

So what did she do? Take a chance on him someday loving her or leave and return to New York?

"Are you going to marry him?" her aunt said.

Ignoring her aunt, she walked over to the tree where he'd hung their Christmas wishes. Picking up the paper tied with string, she read his note:

To make my ranch a home, but above all else for Everleigh to be happy.

He wanted her to be happy? Wasn't that a sign of a man in love, when he put her needs before his own? And didn't all his deeds from the last ten days show a caring man who would feel an obligation toward the people in his life and wanted their happiness and wellbeing above his own. He could say he loved her in actions, just not in words. And why would she give up a man like Seth because he couldn't express with words what his demeanor told her?

Was she being too harsh by putting her need for a verbal confirmation above how he was expressing his love in his actions? And he would be waiting at the altar for her. He was taking a risk, hoping she'd show to marry him at the church after he'd already been stood up once. He had faith in her--in them? Why didn't she?

Maybe she should reconsider and give him a chance.

She loved him. She wanted a life with him. So what was her problem besides those three little words?

CHAPTER 25

Seth Ketchum watched the people milling about the party, his stomach clenched, his throat almost paralyzed with fear. He was either the biggest fool or the stupidest man alive. Yesterday, when he faced Everleigh, he'd meant to tell her he loved her, he wanted her to be his wife, but he'd stood there in front of her aunt and uncle and froze. He'd told her everything but the most important details as to why she should marry him. And today he wouldn't be a bit surprised if she didn't show up. He couldn't blame her.

After all, they both wanted marriages like their parents, where they loved their partners heart and soul. And yet he couldn't spit out those three important words.

Every woman dreamed of a proposal. Well, today, if Everleigh appeared, he'd fulfill her dreams. He had it all planned out.

"Big day," Bart said to him, clapping him on the back of his shoulder.

"Yes," he said, barely able to talk. He kept watching the door, waiting, hoping, praying she'd appear.

The party had been going for quite some time. A big banner

posted in the reception area of the church said, *Thank You, Dr. Callahan.*

From the stories he heard, the doctor had done a remarkable job of saving a lot of lives. An epidemic could wipe out a small town. And yet she'd saved so many to enjoy another Christmas with their loved ones.

He swallowed, trying to calm the nerves that threatened to consume him.

Everleigh walked in the door and his heart squeezed his chest painfully.

"Excuse me," he said to the preacher, as his feet moved toward her like a magnet to steel.

She'd shown up. But was she going to marry him.

Dressed in a simple white dress, she looked beautiful. He hoped the dress was the answer to his prayers.

Grabbing her hands, he dropped to one knee.

"Seth?" she said, her eyes widening.

"Everleigh Walsh, you stormed into my life along with a blizzard, snowing us in together. During those days together, you refused to let me hibernate from life any longer and taught me that I was worthy of love. You wrapped up my heart just like a Christmas present that will never stop giving. You are the missing piece of my heart. I love you more today than I did yesterday and my love will continue to grow. I want with you the kind of love our parents shared. Will you marry me?"

The crowd had grown silent as they watched the couple.

Smiling, though her eyes were filled with tears, Everleigh pulled him to his feet, holding his hands. "I came here today to marry you, not knowing if you loved me or not, but only that your actions showed me what your lips could not say. I came here on faith, hoping you loved me like I love you. But once again, your behavior has proven that you're the man for me. I love you with all my heart, Seth Ketchum, and I'd be honored to be your wife."

The crowd clapped, people cheering.

He ignored everyone around them and pulled her into his arms. "We're getting married."

"I wasn't going to leave a good man like you standing at the altar."

Love flooded his body and he knew he'd found the forever kind of love that his parents shared.

"And I wasn't going to let my scandalous suffragette not fulfill her dreams."

She laughed. "I think I found the most important dream right here in your arms in Mistletoe, Montana. Let's get married. I want to wake up Christmas morning in your arms as your wife."

Want to Read Seth's Parent's Story?

1846 INDIAN TERRITORY

Death spiraled toward the sky in a hazy plume of thick black smoke, spreading its raucous odor across the hilly countryside. From his chestnut mare, Wade Ketchum gazed upon the burned wagons, scattered furniture and littered bodies. The sight seemed unreal in the early morning light, but the woman kneeling beside a freshly dug grave, shoulders shaking with grief, made the scene painfully real.

Wade slid from his saddle, the creak of leather echoing in the deadly quiet. Alert, he walked towards the woman, his boots crunching on the hard ground. As she bent over the grave, her sunbonnet rested against her slender shoulders, exposing a soft mass of mahogany tresses at her nape.

Her head was bowed her hands clasped together.

"Please, Father, I need your help. Guide us through Your wilderness."

Wade hesitated. The woman was praying.

"Send someone to help us. I can't do this alone." She sobbed. "Our lives are in Your hands. Amen."

Wade cleared his throat.

She jumped up, whirling around at the sound. Her gaze collided with his, and her shoulders seemed to sag with relief.

"I was afraid it was the Pawnee returning," she said, her voice filled with relief, her eyes wary of him.

"Are you hurt?"

"No, just terribly frightened," she answered, her voice shaking with suppressed emotion.

Wade glanced at the camp. Smoke drifted across the area giving it a ghostly appearance, nothing stirred. The attack had been recent, and even one survivor was a miracle.

A feeling of unease crept up his spine. Why was she still here, vulnerable to another attack? "What happened?"

"The Pawnee ambushed our wagon train late yesterday evening. I've been trying to hitch up our wagon." She rambled nervously on. "I was beginning to wonder if we were going to all die here in this barren country." The woman held out a shaky right hand. "I'm Rachel Cooke."

"Wade Ketchum, ma'am." Gripping her cold palm, he realized the woman was skittish as a wild horse.

She withdrew her hand from his, wrapping her arms around her middle as if to protect herself. She stared at the destruction of what once had been fifteen or more wagons, and seemed to sag before his eyes. One wagon stood apart from the others, the canvas singed and ripped, but otherwise still intact.

"We were fortunate," she whispered, as a sob escaped her throat. "Somehow our wagon was spared." She wrung her hands fretfully. "But the oxen were spooked by the raid, and I haven't been able to hitch them, to take us away from here."

"Ma'am, I'm surprised you still have oxen."

"They were down at the creek being watered when the attack occurred. We heard the noise and hid in the bushes."

Wade wanted to reach out and touch her, reassure her somehow. Knowing he had to be in Fort Laramie in three days, knowing she would only slow him down, and yet knowing he couldn't leave her behind, he said, "I'll hitch your wagon and help you reach the next town."

"Just get us out of here. Away from all this. I don't care where you're going," she said, her voice trembling with fear.

"I won't leave you, ma'am," Wade said, trying to dispel the fear from her eyes, nervous about the possible return of the Pawnee.

His gazed wandered to the single grave. "Your husband?"

She followed his gaze. "No, it's Miss Cooke. The grave is my father's." She choked up momentarily. "I couldn't stand the thought of animals or Indians desecrating his body. So I spent the morning, burying him the best I could. But the others, God rest their souls, I couldn't help them."

While not a classic beauty, she was pretty, in an unusual way. There was a wholesomeness of face and spirit that Wade was not accustomed to in a woman.

He sneaked another glance, his gaze taking in the delicate profile and lush curves. Those curves would be a definite distraction.

Wade picked up the hitch and approached the oxen. He slipped the yoke around their necks and proceeded to fasten it on the animals. "I have to be in Fort Laramie in three days. I'll take you that far, but then you're on your own."

She wrapped her arms around herself, as if a chill had passed over her. "I'm so grateful you came along. We were on our way to The Dalles, Oregon, to my father's new church."

"You should be able to catch up with another wagon train in Fort Laramie, Miss Cooke. They'll see you on to Oregon." He checked the ropes one last time. "Are you ready? I don't want to linger here any longer than necessary."

"I agree. Just let me get the children," she said.

"Children?" Wade heard himself blurt the word. "I thought you said you weren't married? That no one else survived."

"Just my sister and three orphans. My father was a minister. We ran an orphanage back home, in Tennessee."

Suddenly, a small army crashed through the brush. Wade whirled around and pulled his gun, expecting to face Pawnee and came face-to-face with a beauty. The young woman held a small baby in her arms and a little girl of about seven tugged a freckled-faced adolescent boy behind her. They all stopped, wide eyes fixed on him and his gun.

Wade stared at the group in disbelief. "What the hell?" He shoved the weapon back in his holster.

"Mr. Ketchum, please watch your language!" Rachel exclaimed.

He didn't have time for children. They were little creatures that cried or whined most of the time and had a way of getting under your skin, twisting your heart. He didn't need the aggravation, or the memories they evoked.

The little girl looked wide-eyed at him, and Wade growled, "I don't know, Miss Cooke. I didn't bargain for this."

Catching sight of Rachel, the baby started to fuss, holding out his arms. The young woman carrying the infant grimaced with distaste. She hurried over to Rachel, her long skirts swishing, and shoved the baby into Rachel's arms. "It's your turn to take care of this wet, fussy brat."

With a toss of her blond curls, the other woman informed Rachel, "We couldn't stand waiting in that ravine any longer. The children had to see you were all right."

"I'm fine, Becky. This is Mr. Ketchum. He's going to see us to the next town."

Becky carefully assessed him from head to toe. For a moment he felt like he was sized up, tagged, and numbered. Trouble was etched in her smile, in the way she walked and in every line of her seductive body.

"Nice to meet you, Mr. Ketchum," she cooed.

Wade shook his head in bewilderment. These two women couldn't possibly be sisters. They were about as much alike as a skunk and a porcupine.

"Rachel, the wagons--they're all burned," the little girl cried.

She knelt with the baby on her hip, putting herself at the child's level. "Yes, Grace, I know."

"Where is Papa Cooke?" the child asked.

"Remember what we talked about last night?"

"But I want to see him."

Tears filled Rachel's eyes. "We won't see him again until we get to heaven. Let's say a prayer for Papa and everyone else before we leave."

Wade swore beneath his breath. "Miss Cooke, we don't have time for a prayer service. Those Indians could return any time."

She looked at him the way a schoolmarm would gaze at a misbehaving child.

"Please, Mr. Ketchum, the children and I need just a few moments to say good-bye. We'll make it quick."

How could a woman who looked so soft be so damn stubborn?

He watched Rachel gather her small brood around the lone grave. She pulled a Bible from her apron pocket and read a passage as unfamiliar to him as Greek. Then bowed her head and led them in prayer.

Not for the first time, Wade wondered what he'd gotten himself into. He shook his head, mentally chastising himself for getting involved. Three days from now the biggest card game west of the Mississippi was being played in Fort Laramie, and he intended on winning that money. He had to win a decent amount in that card game or find himself stranded, unable to continue the search for his brother.

But he couldn't just leave them here. And more importantly,

the sight of Miss Cooke bending over that grave had touched a memory he'd rather forget.

"Thank you, Father, for sending us Mr. Ketchum," Rachel said. "Amen."

"Good Lord! Now she thinks I'm a damned saint," Wade mumbled his thoughts out loud.

Immediately, Rachel turned to face Wade, sending him a puzzled look. "What did you say, Mr. Ketchum?"

"I don't have time to cart a bunch of kids around," Wade said, running a hand through his hair as he gazed upon the children. "I have to be in Fort Laramie by Saturday."

Becky twittered with laughter. "Oh, I don't think a strong man like you would leave three small children and two helpless females all alone in the wilderness."

Helpless? Maybe they appeared vulnerable, but any woman who survived an Indian attack and buried a man, was anything but defenseless.

"Mr. Ketchum, I would like to leave here as soon as possible," Rachel asserted suddenly. "Are you going to help us or not?"

Everyone turned to him expectantly. Only the baby seemed uninterested in his response. The blonde-haired little girl looked so much like his sister Sarah, her gaze felt like a knife gouging his heart. They were wasting precious time.

He cursed under his breath."Of course, I'm going to help you. But I'm not going to spend another minute waiting for the damn Pawnee to return. Let's go."

Available At Amazon!

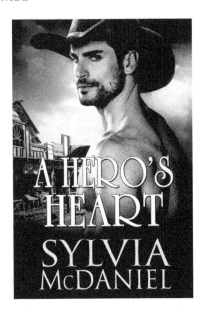

Eugenia Meets Her Match! Come Spend Christmas With The Burnett Family.

Chapter One

"June told me you're good at helping a woman find a husband," Myrtle Sanders said, her voice soft and barely discernible over the clank of dishes and customers' voices in the café in Fort Worth, Texas.

Eugenia Burnett's ears were hurting from the last hour of Myrtle's continuous whining about how her children didn't visit her and how loneliness was her only companion.

Her story had begun to grate on Eugenia's nerves like ants scurrying along a trail until she was ready to tell the woman she had to run. Literally, she wanted to escape.

Finally, like an overdue stagecoach, the conversation seemed to have arrived at the reason Myrtle had asked her to lunch.

"Much to my children's dismay, I do enjoy dabbling in helping people find a partner," Eugenia admitted, her mind already thinking of the possible matches for Myrtle. She'd find her a man.

Eugenia smiled, her heart warming at the thought of her sons and their families. Since she'd found mates for her three stubborn boys, she'd begun to help her friends find people to spend the rest of their days with.

The woman smiled, her eyes full of doubt. "What's the chance of either one of us ever marrying again?"

"Me?" Eugenia asked, stunned. What had she said that gave this woman the impression she wanted a husband? She needed to disavow this notion immediately.

"I'm not looking to get hitched to any man. I don't need the aggravation of being married. I'm in a mighty nice place. My kids are close. The ranch is run by Travis and Tanner, and I have spending money if I need it. There is nothing that a man can provide that I need."

When Thomas died, the ranch was earning enough she could continue her style of life without her husband. Without a man telling her when to take her next breath.

"Not even companionship?" the woman asked, a pensive pinch to her face.

Eugenia shrugged, remembering those first few desolate nights. "If I get lonely, my grandchildren are close-by. The rest of the time is mine to do what I please."

Myrtle shook her head. "My Charlie use to wrap his arms around me at night and hold me close. I miss that tenderness."

"He also liked to tell you what you could and couldn't do," Eugenia said, remembering how Thomas ordered her around. She was no longer that pliant bride of fifteen.

"Yes, men seem to think they have to be in control of a woman," Myrtle admitted.

"And I don't need any man to tell me what I can and can't do. I'm quite capable of taking care of myself."

Long gone were the days when Eugenia Burnett took orders from any man. Now she was a strong woman capable of voicing her opinion and making her own decisions.

Myrtle sighed. "Sometimes Charlie was a little overbearing, but there were times I could change his mind. At this age, a good man is hard to find. I'm lonely. I don't like living by myself. I want a man to take care of me."

"Don't worry. I'm certain I can help you. Just last month I helped Claudine meet Richard. I also introduced Mary to Loyd and then there was June and Dillon. Women our age can find a man if we want one," Eugenia assured Myrtle.

Though the sparkle of youth had faded, Eugenia's friends claimed they were lonely and needed mates at their sides. Matching up widow women entertained her and kept her busy, much to her sons' dislike.

Myrtle leaned in closer. "You certainly like to match people up. I mean look at your sons. You put them together with their wives."

"Someone had to, or I would never have had any grandkids. They didn't seem inclined to find women to settle down with, so I took action to get what I wanted. Grandkids. Now I have two boys and a girl with another one on the way."

"You are a determined woman."

Eugenia almost laughed out loud. Now she was a determined woman, but in her youth…she'd been a milquetoast bride. Not any longer.

"I go after what I want, and most of the time I get my way." Eugenia lifted her chin defiantly. Since Thomas passed away, she'd relished in her freedom. She'd grown strong and hard as nails and wielded her matriarchal power over her sons.

"Myrtle, what do you want? Do you want another man telling you what to do?" Eugenia asked.

"I want someone by my side. I want to roll over in the middle of the night and reach out to feel a man beside me. I want to smile across the dinner table and have someone to talk to."

The noise from the café seemed to fade into the background as Eugenia stared at Myrtle's brown hair streaked with strands of gray and her milky complexion lined with wrinkles.

"Let me think about who is available," Eugenia said as she

thought of the eligible widowers and single men in town that she knew. "Red Jenkins's wife just died, so it's too soon for him. James Randall has been a widower for six months, but he has a fondness for drink. Bart Smith has been a widower for a year, but his children still live with him. You would be taking on the care of two older kids. Then there is Wyatt Jones. He was married to my friend Beatrice."

Eugenia's heart quivered at the thought of big Wyatt.

"I know Wyatt. He's one big cowboy. One that certainly makes a woman's heart flutter," Myrtle said, her blue eyes wide and dreamy with the possibility.

Eugenia nodded her head. Yes, she thought so, too. "He's quite the catch. A mite stubborn, but he took great care of Beatrice when she was ill. Wyatt's all bullheaded man."

Myrtle whispered softly. "What would you recommend I do?"

"Simple. Make him a casserole dish and take it out to his place. After all, it's just him and the ranch hands. As far as I know, he doesn't have anyone making him home-cooked meals. Men love a good meal."

Men were so gullible. A home-cooked meal and the romance was on.

Myrtle grinned, her blue eyes shining with tears. "Charlie always loved my chicken and rice. Do I just drop it off?"

"Sure. It's a signal that you're interested in him. You take him the casserole, you smile, and you tell him you hope to see him in town soon. That's a subtle way of saying you'd like him to ask you out to dinner. If he doesn't respond, then you try again."

Myrtle stared at her, a frown creased her forehead. "What if he just stares at me? What do I do then?"

"Oh, he's smart enough to know what you're implying. If he doesn't respond by the second casserole, then we'll have to find someone else."

And Wyatt had turned down more than one casserole she'd sent his way. Sooner or later, he would take the bait.

Myrtle frowned, her eyes wrinkling in the corners. "You're sure about this?"

"It's how Mary and Loyd met."

The door to the café opened, the cold wind slamming it against the wall. The restaurant grew quiet with the sudden entrance, and Eugenia turned to see who was making such a racket.

Wyatt Jones stood in the doorway, his muscular frame filling the opening. His cowboy hat sat at an angle on top of his head, and his large brown eyes scanned the room.

In his hand, he carried a duffle bag.

Eugenia tried to ignore the big man as he strolled through the door. As he stepped inside the café, he removed his Stetson.

Their gazes locked across the room, and he smiled, his full lips turning up in a grin that made her body soften and her heart give an extra little *ca-thunk*. He spoke to the waitress, but his gaze never wavered from Eugenia.

Uh-oh. A tingle of nerves zinged through her bones. This couldn't be good.

His boots made a rhythmic thump, thump, thump on the wooden floor as he walked with a determined stride straight toward her, his bag in hand, his spurs jingling. Nervously, she licked her lips.

Myrtle's back faced the door, and she continued to blather about something. But Eugenia couldn't seem to focus on the words. All she could see was this handsome cowboy walking her way. She couldn't stop staring at him. She knew he was coming for her.

She'd already sent several women his way, and she didn't think he was here to thank her for curing his loneliness.

Wyatt stopped at their table, touching the rim of his hat as he glanced at Myrtle. "Morning Mrs. Sanders. Nice to see you."

He pivoted to Eugenia, his brown eyes dancing with merriment. Staring into those earthy brown eyes, a warm flush settled over her like a blanket. He opened the bag, withdrew a casserole dish, and laid it on the table. He took a second dish out and placed it alongside the first one, and then another, and another.

Oh dear.

When he finished, six clean, empty casserole dishes sat in front of her.

His mouth turned up in that slow, lazy grin that burned a sizzle along her spine. Why did this man make her feel like she'd raced her grandchildren around the yard and couldn't catch her breath? Why did this man make her more nervous than a virgin on her wedding day? Why did this man have her wondering how his lips would feel against her own?

"Eugenia," he said in that deep drawl that sent shivers skittering over her. "You've been mighty busy, sending women out to my house. You've kept me and my men well fed the last couple of weeks."

"Glad I could help," she said, her voice sounding breathy and soft.

He leaned in close and put his hands on either side of her, effectively pinning her in the chair. She felt the urge to jump up and run, but resisted. She sat there, stared him in the eye and refused to back down. No longer would she back down to any man.

"While I appreciate the effort, I'm not taking the bait. There's only one woman in this town that I'm interested in pursuing to become my wife." The deep timbre of his voice was low and commanding.

"And pray tell, who would that be?" she asked, knowing she would have him hitched as soon as possible.

"You, Eugenia Burnett. You."

His cinnamon eyes twinkled with amusement and left her tingly in places she refused to acknowledge.

The heat from the fireplace warmed the room, but she sat

frozen in her chair, unable to move, unable to respond. Wyatt Jones wanted her to become his wife?

"Think about it."

Before her mouth began to work again, he rose, picked up his bag, turned, and walked out of the restaurant.

Slowly her body seemed to come to life again and with it her resolve. He'd be waiting until hell froze over if he thought she would marry him.

Inside the Burnett homestead kitchen, Rose Burnett glanced around the table at her sisters-in-law. Eugenia was outside playing with Lucas and Desiree while the women had a rare moment alone.

"Hey, did y'all hear what happened at the cafe?"

Sarah started to laugh. "Did I hear? Tucker came in laughing about how his mother may have finally met her match."

Beth looked confused. "What happened?"

Rose and Sarah told her how Wyatt Jones had confronted Eugenia at the café.

"He said he wanted to marry her?" Rose asked, her voice low.

"Said she was the only woman he was interested in pursuing is what I heard," Sarah replied.

Beth about snorted her coffee. "Wow! I don't know how Tanner would feel about his mother remarrying. How about Tucker and Travis?"

Rose smiled. "Oh, Travis thinks his mother needs someone to keep her under control. Since she lied to bring us together and said I stole her wedding ring, he's thinking maybe she needs someone to make certain she minds her own business."

Though Rose was grateful to Eugenia for bringing them together, during that time, Travis had made her life miserable.

Sarah rolled her eyes. "The way she lied to me about my

grandfather being ill. It's very hard to believe everything she says. I know she brought me home with the hope that Tucker and I would work out our differences." She rubbed her hand across her swollen stomach. "I'm glad that she did, but when I got off that stage and learned that grandfather wasn't seriously ill, I would have gladly strangled that woman."

"I never would have met Tanner if it wasn't for her," Beth acknowledged quietly. "Though I almost wound up with Tucker, now I'm grateful to her."

"Yes, but don't you think she deserves the same happiness that we have with our husbands?" Rose asked, thinking that her mother-in-law deserved her own chance at happiness. "Her husband's been dead for well over five years. It would be better for her to have a man she could focus her attention on rather than her sons."

"And grandchildren," Beth said.

"And matchmaking. You did hear that she has sent six women to Wyatt's place with casserole dishes," Sarah volunteered.

Rose giggled like a young girl, thinking of Eugenia's reaction to Wyatt's casserole dish display. The gossip had spread faster than cholera through town. "I would love to have witnessed her reaction when Wyatt laid out all those empty casserole dishes in front of her."

"Has she mentioned Wyatt? Do you think she's interested in getting married again?" Beth asked.

Sarah shook her head. "Oh no, she wants nothing to do with getting married herself. She told Tucker at dinner the other night that there was no way that she would saddle herself with another husband. One was enough."

There was a group sigh, and for a moment everyone sat there in silence. Finally, Beth said, "Did either of you want to get married?"

The other two women shook their heads.

"No way," Rose responded, remembering her dreams of being like her mother, an actress on the stage.

"Not really," Sara replied. "I had my son and my practice, what more could I need?"

"Yet, when we fell in love, we wanted to marry our husbands," Rose said.

"And how did we meet our husbands?" Beth asked.

"Eugenia," the three women responded in unison. They laughed.

"How do we help her fall in love?" Rose asked, trying to remember when she realized she loved Travis. They had fought each other and the feeling for so long that when they finally succumbed, it was euphoric.

Sara grinned. "We do what Mama Burnett did. Every chance we get, we wrangle them together."

Rose leaned back and laughed. Eugenia wouldn't let Travis arrest her again, so she'd stayed at the ranch because of Eugenia. "Wyatt hasn't been to the ranch recently. We'll invite him for dinner next weekend. Beth and I will plan everything, and you and Tucker can come out. The whole family will get to meet Mr. Jones."

"You know, there's the annual Christmas tree event coming up soon. Let's do everything we can to arrange for them to be in the same wagon," Beth said, laughing gleefully.

"The meeting about the Christmas pageant is in two weeks. Eugenia said she was going to volunteer again to be the pageant director," Sarah said, unable to contain a giggle.

"But this year, Mr. Davis passed away. They need a new coordinator. Wonder if we can convince Wyatt he would make an excellent organizer," Rose said excitedly.

They laughed.

Sara nodded at her sisters-in-law. "Sometimes what we do can come back to haunt us. This time Eugenia is going to meet her match."

Rose nodded, thinking poor Eugenia was going to get quite a surprise. "This time we're doing the matchmaking."

Wyatt looked over at Gus, his ranch foreman, the man who'd been at his side for nearly twenty years. Since Beatrice's death, Wyatt had taken to eating in the bunkhouse with the men rather than up at the large, empty house he rumbled around in.

After dinner, he and Gus usually came back to the house where they would share a whiskey or two before they each headed off to bed.

"It's December, and already that north wind is colder than a well-digger's ass in Montana," Gus said, backing up to the blaze, warming his backside.

Tonight was cold, and Wyatt had started a fire in the hearth to chase the chill from the study. He'd refused to let Beatrice decorate this one room. This room belonged to him, and he'd decorated it just the way he damn well pleased. Now, he wanted to move his bed in here rather than sleep in that lonely bedroom upstairs. He missed his wife, the healthy Beatrice, not the woman who'd wasted away before his eyes.

"Yes, we probably need to have the men go ahead and move the cattle to the south pasture, where we can keep an eye on them. Looks like winter arrived early this year."

Books graced the shelves along with liquor bottles. Above the fireplace mantel hung his ten-point buck he'd shot right after they built the house. This house, his home, held so many memories, and now he was ready to create more memories with someone, maybe even Eugenia.

"Yap," Gus responded and then rubbed his belly. "I was getting spoilt to those casseroles you kept bringing out. What happened? They've dried up worse than the creek in summer."

"I put an end to them," Wyatt responded, remembering the

look on Eugenia's face as he'd pulled out the empty dishes. Sometimes a man had to get the upper hand, and he'd taken the first step that day.

"Dang, I was enjoying a woman's cooking for a change."

"Then I'll give you the women's names and you can call on them," Wyatt admonished, taking a swig of his drink.

Gus rolled his eyes. "And end up hog tied to one of 'em? No, thanks. You're used to a woman, and since Miss Beatrice has been gone a year, maybe you should consider one of these fine ladies who are cooking you casseroles."

Wyatt set his glass down and considered his friend. Funny how a man who'd never married could give him advice on finding a woman. "The problem is that none of them interest me."

"Dang, that's a real shame. I was enjoying their cooking. Could you at least string them along for a little while, so we can continue to eat decent food?"

Wyatt slammed his drink on the desk. "Now, what kind of man does that to a woman?"

Gus was a great foreman, a good man who didn't know how to handle women. Never had been able to keep a woman interested in him longer than a courting moon. Maybe there was a reason he'd never married.

"A hungry man?"

"Go to the damn café if you're hungry. Don't depend on widow women who are looking husbands, unless you want to get hitched," Wyatt told him.

"No, thanks!" Gus held up his hand and shook his head. "You have to admit we haven't had food like that since Mrs. Beatrice died."

Beatrice had been an excellent cook. They'd eaten well, and her pies were known for bringing the men running in from the barn. But she was gone. "Well, it's over. I put a stop to the widow women's cooking."

Gus sank into a chair across from him and laughed. "Why did all these women think you were on the hunt for a wife?"

"From what I was told, they were sent here by Eugenia Burnett." He couldn't help but think about Eugenia. Her dark hair was more silver than black, and her blue eyes sparkled with heat and laughter. For being almost fifty, her figure was still neat and trim in a shorter spitfire version.

"Mrs. Beatrice's friend?"

"The one." The woman was a small ball of dynamite that no one wanted to cross.

Gus stammered in shock. "Wweell why would she be trying to set up her friend's husband?"

Wyatt shrugged and contemplated the fire. "You know we often had Eugenia and Thomas out for dinner."

Eugenia and he shared something that they had never acknowledged while they were both married. At a dinner, they'd accidentally touched, and Wyatt's body had tingled and hummed with something he'd never experienced before. While he was married to Beatrice, he'd avoided his wife's best friend.

"Yes, those two women could talk the feathers off a chicken."

Wyatt took a sip of his whiskey, letting it warm him all the way to his toes, just like a fine woman could heat up a man. And that's what he missed. He missed having a woman. Her soft touches, tender smiles, and gentle reminders. It was the little things that he took for granted.

He missed having a strong-willed woman who would stand up to him and challenge him to become a better man.

After spending the day around men, he missed coming home to a woman's voice, her smell, the way she eased his burdens.

"You haven't answered my question. Why is Eugenia trying to find you a wife?"

"Maybe because when our mates were alive, there was always this mindfulness between us. Nothing ever happened of course, but we felt drawn to one another."

Nothing ever happened, but now that Beatrice had been gone a year, he wanted to set fire to that ember in Eugenia. There was something there that he wanted to create a blazing inferno with. Even thinking about her made his gut tighten and blood rush to his groin.

Gus's brows rose as he looked at Wyatt over his drink. "Are you crazy? That woman is known for her meddling. They call her the meddling matchmaker. Why in the hell Eugenia? Why not some sensible woman?"

Wyatt leaned toward Gus. "Oh, Eugenia's sensible all right. She's strong willed and wouldn't cower every time I raised my voice to her like most women. Give me a woman who knows what she wants and goes after her desires rather than one who lays around with the damn vapors all day."

"Beatrice—"

"Beatrice was great until she got sick. Then all I could do was sit by and watch her waste away. Both of us died a little bit every day. Her body and my heart. But she's gone."

Three years of being ill and then she'd gone like a thief in the night, quiet and quick, leaving behind her grief-stricken family. Now over twelve months had passed, and he was ready to move on.

"God rest her soul." Gus raised his glass in the air to Beatrice and then put it to his lips and gulped. "Still, you and Eugenia Burnett. I'm so damn shocked I can't feel my face anymore."

"You can't feel your face because of the whiskey."

"That too. But Eugenia? Slap me upside the head. You've got your spurs tangled up. Is she interested in you?"

Wyatt shrugged. "Who knows? I told her she was the only woman I wanted to get a casserole from."

"She hasn't brought one yet," Gus said.

Oh, Eugenia Burnett would not be that easy. No, courting Eugenia would be tricky and so much fun.

"She's not going to, either. It's going to take a little more persuasion on my part before she'll come around. Eugenia's not some young filly ready to be bred. Nope, she's going to require some top-notch courting."

Gus started laughing. "The idea of you courting a woman at your age is pretty funny."

"That better be the whiskey talking. I'm still young enough to want a woman in my bed. I'm still young enough that I don't want some wimpy woman who is just going to lie there and endure. Eugenia will make a great wife. She'll make life interesting again."

"Lord, boss, if she's what you want, I hope you're right. If not, you're going to spend the rest of your days living in marriage hell."

"Or it could be damn near heaven."

Available At All Retailers!

LEAVE A REVIEW

Did you enjoy Mistletoe Scandal? Reviews help authors and are very much appreciated.

Join the new book alerts at www.SylviaMcDaniel.com

Join the Facebook Group and hang out with us!

Psst...don't forget to follow me on Bookbub.

Also By Sylvia McDaniel
Western Historicals
A Hero's Heart
Second Chance Cowboy
Ethan

American Brides
**Katie: Bride of Virginia

Angel Creek Christmas Brides
**Charity
**Ginger
**Minne
**Cora

Bad Girls of the West
Scandalous Sadie
Ravenous Rose
Tempting Tessa
Nellie's Redemption

The Burnett Brides Series
The Rancher Takes A Bride
The Outlaw Takes A Bride
The Marshal Takes A Bride
The Christmas Bride
Boxed Set

Lipstick and Lead Series
Desperate
Deadly
Dangerous

143

Daring
**Determined
Deceived
Defiant
Devious
Lipstick and Lead Box Set Books 1-4
Lipstick and Lead Box Set Books 5-9
Lipstick and Lead Box Set Books 1-9
**Quinlan's Quest

Mail Order Bride Tales
**A Brother's Betrayal
**Pearl
**Ace's Bride

Scandalous Suffragettes of the West
**Abigail
Bella
Mistletoe Scandal

Southern Historical Romance
A Scarlet Bride

The Cuvier Women
Wronged
Betrayed
Beguiled
Boxed Set

The Debutante's of Durango
The Debutante's Scandal
The Debutante's Gamble
The Debutante's Revenge
The Debutante's Santa

** Denotes a sweet book.

Want to learn about my new releases before anyone else? Sign up for my New Book Alert and receive a complimentary book.

USA Today Best-selling author, Sylvia McDaniel obviously has too much time on her hands. With over seventy western historical and contemporary romance novels, she spends most days torturing her characters. Bad boys deserve punishment and even good girls get into trouble. Always looking for the next plot twist, she's known for her sweet, funny, family-oriented romances.

Married to her best friend for over twenty-five years, they recently moved to the state of Colorado where they like to hike, and enjoy the beauty of the forest behind their home with their spoiled dachshund Zeus and puppy Bailey. (He has his own column in her newsletter.)

Their grown son, still lives in Texas. An avid football watcher, she loves the Broncos and the Cowboys, especially when they're winning.

www.SylviaMcDaniel.com
Sylvia@SylviaMcDaniel.com
The End!

91687921R00085